Books in the M.I. High series:

M.I. High: A New Generation
M.I. High: Secrets and Spies
The Official M.I. High Spy Survival Handbook

# M.I.HIGH

## A New Generation

**Adapted by Jonny Zucker**

**PUFFIN**

PUFFIN BOOKS

Published by the Penguin Group
Penguin Books Ltd, 80 Strand, London WC2R 0RL, England
Penguin Group (USA) Inc., 375 Hudson Street, New York, New York 10014, USA
Penguin Group (Canada), 90 Eglinton Avenue East, Suite 700, Toronto, Ontario, Canada M4P 2Y3
(a division of Pearson Penguin Canada Inc.)
Penguin Ireland, 25 St Stephen's Green, Dublin 2, Ireland (a division of Penguin Books Ltd)
Penguin Group (Australia), 250 Camberwell Road, Camberwell, Victoria 3124, Australia
(a division of Pearson Australia Group Pty Ltd)
Penguin Books India Pvt Ltd, 11 Community Centre, Panchsheel Park, New Delhi – 110 017, India
Penguin Group (NZ), 67 Apollo Drive, Rosedale, North Shore 0632, New Zealand
(a division of Pearson New Zealand Ltd)
Penguin Books (South Africa) (Pty) Ltd, 24 Sturdee Avenue, Rosebank,
Johannesburg 2196, South Africa

Penguin Books Ltd, Registered Offices: 80 Strand, London WC2R 0RL, England

puffinbooks.com

First published in Puffin Books 2007
1

Text copyright © Keith Brumpton and Kudos Film & Television Limited, 2007
Photographs copyright © Kudos Film & Television Limited, 2007
BBC and the BBC logo are the trademarks of the British Broadcasting Corporation
and are used under licence. BBC logo © BBC 1996.
Text adapted by Jonny Zucker
All rights reserved

Set in Helvetica Neue
Typeset by Palimpsest Book Production Limited,
Grangemouth, Stirlingshire

Made and printed in England by Clays Ltd, St Ives plc

British Library Cataloguing in Publication Data
A CIP catalogue record for this book is available from the British Library

ISBN: 978-0-141-32361-9

# Contents

# The Sinister
# Prime Minister

# Chapter 1

The Guinea Pig slipped the Control Helmet over her deformed ears, until its visor rested snugly on her fur-covered snout. Her hands were trembling slightly, her heart racing in anticipation of the impending experiment. If today's prototype trial went well, her dream would soon become a reality. The scientific world would never mock her again. Instead, they would be at *her* mercy.

She surveyed her dimly-lit underground laboratory. NOSE – the National Organization for Scientific Exploration – had shut down her original lab nearly ten years earlier, after they had deemed her self-experimentation methods 'unethical'. Narrow-minded fools! But she had slowly built up these secret headquarters, deep beneath a disused East End warehouse. A place where her evil genius could blossom undisturbed.

All around her sprawled the evidence of her scientific toil – dismembered test dummies with cables sprouting from their severed heads and limbs; patches of synthetic skin and clumps of hair; an artificial eyeball connected to a complex bundle of electrical wires. It had been a long, hard haul to get to this point – but now she was almost ready.

The Guinea Pig turned to the chessboard on the workbench before her. A disembodied hand hovered over the chess-piece armies expectantly, its only attachment a snaking cluster of wires.

As she focused her mind, the scientist could almost feel the Control Helmet tracing the neural impulses.

'Yes!' she hissed enthusiastically, as the hand grasped the white queen and drove it forwards, crashing it into a black pawn. 'Good, good! That's it!'

She watched with glee as the hand responded by plucking the fallen pawn from the board, then clenching into a fist around it.

'Now destroy!'

The hand's grip tightened, effortlessly crushing the chess piece. As fine black powder trickled through its fingers to the chessboard, the Guinea Pig let out a wild burst of ecstatic laughter.

A few more refinements, then the device would be ready. She would have control of the world's ultimate weapon. The people who had ridiculed and exiled her would be helpless in her grasp.

And she would crush them like pawns.

# Chapter 2

She might have been one of St Hope's most popular teachers, but that didn't mean Ms Templeman's Year Nine students were ever interested in trying to learn anything in her classes. Despite a very exciting lesson drawn from the pages of *Practical Science*, the pretty teacher could see from all the yawning, stretching and whispers that today was going to be an uphill battle. Nonetheless, she valiantly carried on with her lesson, her colourful bangles jangling on her wrists.

'Cell division is not the only means by which organisms can replicate themselves . . .'

Of course, there *were* exceptions. Ms Templeman glanced at Rose Gupta, sitting attentively in the front row. Now *there* was a girl with a lot going on up top. The teacher could tell her star pupil was trying hard to concentrate on the task at hand. She was the only pupil at St Hope's to stick to the school uniform guidelines, and it was clear Rose had the highest possible standards. Her regulation cardigan was neatly buttoned up, her tie was perfectly knotted and, with her tidy dark hair pulled back in a headband to stop it

5

falling over her glasses, it was obvious she was putting the same measured effort into ignoring the distractions of everyone around her.

If only for Rose's sake, Ms Templeman must rise above the chattering rabble. She must persevere.

'Now consider, for example, the varied reproductive cycle of the sea cucumber. *Holothuria Scabra* . . . I'll write that down.'

Rose diligently copied the Latin name into her notes. Science held a fascination for Rose and it was a mystery why most of her classmates didn't share her enthusiasm – why most of them knew the music charts inside out, but thought the periodic table was something chemists sat round.

Rose's concentration was rudely broken as a ball of scrunched-up paper hit her squarely on the back of the head. Turning, she saw Julian Hamley – better known as Fifty Pence, the self-styled gangsta rapper of St Hope's – leering at her. He was sprawled lazily across his chair, feet on his desk, at the very back of the class. As always, he was sporting a baseball cap, hoodie and chunky gold neckchain. His two devout cronies, Too Cool and Ring Tone, egged him on.

Ms Templeman, however, was too caught up in the exciting world of cloning to notice the ball flying across the room.

Rose sighed inwardly. If any proof were needed that man was descended from the apes, Fifty Pence was it. As he continued to smirk at her, she cast him a withering look.

'Yes, Neanderthal Man can make things fly. Him *very* clever!'

Predictably, Rose's put-down was lost on Fifty Pence and his moronic crew. They didn't do irony. The moment she turned back to her work, a barrage of paper missiles rained down upon her.

'. . . page sixty-four,' Ms Templeman continued, still gallantly pushing on with her biology lesson. 'Cloning is the ability to form exact copies . . .'

The only other pupil showing the least bit of interest in the teacher's monologue was a blond-haired, bright-eyed boy sitting across from Fifty Pence – Stewart Critchley.

'Forget sea cucumbers,' whispered Stewart to his neighbour, a dark-haired boy who was slouched in his chair, clearly not enjoying being stuck in the stuffy classroom. 'The aliens are already here, cloning *humans*. They've got an army of super-beings ready to take over the Earth.'

Blane Whittaker smiled wryly at his best mate's latest crazy notion. He'd known Stewart since primary school, and was well used to his crackpot ideas about conspiracy theories. One of the things he liked best about Stewart was that his conversation was rarely dull. Mental – yes. But not dull.

In the central row of desks, a gang of three girls sat side by side. Their appearance was in stark contrast to that of their classmate Rose. For Daisy Millar and her closest friends, Kaleigh and Zara, fashion was *everything*. A boring compulsory uniform represented a challenge to be overcome by creative accessorizing.

Daisy sat between her two friends – appropriately, as she liked to be at the centre of things. Today, she had opted for a bright yellow T-shirt over her school shirt, heavy green eyeshadow, some serious nail-painting and a radical hairstyle change (one of many). Her latest style experiment saw her honey-coloured hair gelled up on the top of her head in a kind of 1950s' pastiche.

'So? What do you think of the new hair?'

'Cute,' grinned Kaleigh approvingly.

'Yeah,' agreed Zara, 'and, like, totally individual–istical.'

Daisy gave a satisfied smirk. It was nice to see her recent efforts in the coiffure department were appreciated.

At the front of the class, Ms Templeman was soldiering on.

'Cloning has been in the news a lot recently . . .'

As she continued to battle against the hubbub, Rose took down every word, Blane listened to Stewart rave about his latest computer game, and Daisy checked her nails for any signs of varnish damage.

Three very different classmates, with little in common.

Or perhaps not . . .

# Chapter 3

Outside the classroom, Lenny Bicknall, the school's caretaker, was sweeping up leaves. Everyone liked Lenny, but no one took much notice of him as he carried out his business around the school, dressed in a filthy brown jacket and old woolly hat.

He flicked open the end of his broom handle, revealing a small red button, which he then pressed firmly. Seemingly satisfied, Lenny gathered up his tools and headed back inside.

In a second, the eraser end of Rose's pencil began to emit a red pulse of light. Rose quickly covered the light with her hand and looked around to see if anyone else had noticed it. Looking over, she saw Daisy and Blane's pencils were also flashing red.

Rose, Daisy and Blane were being summoned. All three students had to get out of their science class *immediately*.

Their flashing pencils weren't made from ordinary wood and lead. They were, in fact, hi-tech audio-transmitting devices, otherwise known as Pencil Communicators. And their owners simply had to answer the call.

Blane was the first to raise his hand.

'Er, M-Miss . . .' he stuttered, thinking wildly. 'I've got my community liaison lesson!'

Blane was relieved to see Ms Templeman's face light up. He knew he'd said exactly the right thing. His teacher thought the world of students who were happy to help those less fortunate than they were.

'That's very thoughtful of you, Blane.'

Smiling sweetly, Blane added that he helped an OAP on his estate sometimes, receiving yet another approving nod. He grabbed his things and ran for the door. That was almost too easy.

Next in line was Daisy. As the undisputed champion of the school drama queens, she knew she could do better than Blane. Daisy quickly pulled her most pained expression and threw her hand to her forehead for extra effect. It worked a treat and the look of alarm from Kaleigh and Zara was priceless!

'Daisy, are you all right?' asked Ms Templeman, quite worried.

'Miss . . .' Daisy trembled like she'd spent a week in the hospital already. 'Can I be excused too? I've just got this *awful* migraine.'

As Ms Templeman hurried Daisy out the door in the direction of the school nurse, Rose desperately tried to think up a good excuse for leaving. She was hopeless at lying, and, anyway, she was really enjoying this lesson. Still, her secret-agent work came first.

'Miss . . .' Rose's mind spun, trying to think of

anything but the 'loo clause'. That was the one excuse the *Secret Agent Handbook* specifically warned them *not* to use. The only problem was, it was the only one she could remember. She winced as she spoke. 'I, er . . . need the toilet . . .'

Ms Templeman's face fell as she realized she was about to lose the only student who had any genuine interest in the class.

'I had thought *you* at least would be interested in the reproductive cycle of sea cucumbers?' Ms Templeman looked wounded.

'I *am*.' Rose got to her feet. 'I'll be right back,' she promised.

*Phew!*

She broke into a run the moment she got into the corridor. She knew the others would be waiting for her, and she was right. Racing across the school, she found Blane and Daisy standing impatiently by the lockers and in front of an old door, covered in peeling blue paint. On it was a sign that said 'Caretaker's Storeroom'.

Checking there was no one watching them, Daisy carefully slid aside a panel at the front of the light-switch by the door to reveal a white square pad containing three buttons. The top one glowed red, and Daisy pressed it.

*Bzzzz! Ping, ping! Ding dong!*

Blane and Rose waited as Daisy's thumbprint was being scanned until finally a green light appeared. She turned the door handle – they were inside!

Even though the storeroom was cluttered, Rose knew exactly what to do. She reached for the mop in the corner, which turned out to be a lever. This triggered a flashing green arrow on the front of an old paint tin, pointing towards the floor. Before they knew it, there was a great rumbling and the shelves of the storeroom started shaking violently. This was it!

All of a sudden, the room fell completely silent. And then, just as quickly, there was a single *ping!* before all three St Hope's pupils were sent hurtling downwards at death-defying speed.

As you might have guessed by now, the caretaker's storeroom wasn't all it seemed. And if anyone at the school could have seen what was happening to Rose, Daisy and Blane, it's unlikely they would have believed it. Even though it wasn't the kind of fancy door you might imagine when you think of the entrance to the headquarters of secret agents, that's *exactly* what the old blue door with peeling paint was. And right now, the three students were being transported to the very depths of St Hope's School – to M.I. High headquarters.

By the time Rose, Daisy and Blane had reached the bottom of the lift shaft, they'd been transformed into top-secret M.I.9 spies. Gone were the dull old St Hope's uniforms, replaced by sleek black shirts, leather jackets and smart trousers.

The three surveyed the cavernous room as they

strode confidently out of the lift. They could see blue and white spotlights, three plasma TV screens that were part of a large workspace directly in front of them and a series of metal pipes running along the ceiling. And among all the gadgets and black and silver hi-tech equipment, Lenny the caretaker was waiting for them.

Only now, Lenny wasn't wearing his brown jacket and woolly hat. Instead, he was decked out in a fine purple suit, crisp white shirt and purple polka-dot tie. Rose's heart sank as she noticed the stopwatch in Lenny's hand. He wasn't smiling.

'Too slow, too slow!' he chided, pressing the button on the timekeeper. 'And *none* out of ten for that exit strategy, Rose. That's the third time in a row you've used the toilet routine.'

Rose sighed and promised to try harder next time, but Lenny was unimpressed. It wasn't *her* fault she didn't want to lie about helping old people, and she knew any attempts at pretending to be sick would just look silly. She'd have to do some brainstorming on that one.

'Well, maybe if we had a real mission,' Blane cut in sulkily, annoyed with Lenny for telling them off, 'instead of just training all the time.'

Lenny looked at the only male spy in the M.I. High trio and raised an eyebrow.

'You *have* got a real mission,' he said mysteriously. 'This is what we've been preparing you for.'

Rose, Daisy and Blane looked at each other in disbelief. *Wicked!* Trying hard to control their excitement, they listened carefully as Lenny continued.

'M.I.9's concerns are growing about the Prime Minister,' said Lenny, suddenly becoming quite serious. 'At a recent summit he pronounced a new desire to make Britain great again. Take a look at this.'

Turning to one of the large TV screens, Lenny flicked the remote to reveal an image of the British Prime Minister, addressing a press conference in front of a large map of Europe. In each country stood a miniature flag bearing the unmistakable red, white and blue colours of the Union Jack.

'I envisage a new Europe,' the Prime Minister began, staring down the camera. 'One in which Britain and Britain alone shall rule!'

Shouts and questions sounded from reporters in the background as the cruel, cold eyes of the nation's leader stared from the screen.

Lenny pressed the 'pause' button on the remote and looked back at the three students standing before him.

'M.I.9 are afraid he may be about to invade Europe, launching us into World War Three.'

'Why would he do that?' asked Blane, feeling completely confused. It just didn't add up . . .

'*That's* what we want you to find out,' said Lenny dramatically. 'I've pulled a few strings . . . and the PM will be visiting St Hope's – today!'

The three secret spy agents couldn't believe it.

Their first assignment, and it was going to happen right under the noses of their teachers and friends at St Hope's! But how on earth were they ever going to keep their spy identities a secret?

# Chapter 4

It was a pitiful sight. Those with any energy left were half-heartedly filling in their sudoku puzzles or dreaming of the summer break as they flicked through *Holiday in the Sun* brochures. But mostly there were rows of heads fighting to stay awake as they nodded to their chests, the odd snore or snuffle punctuating the air. No, this wasn't a scene from a retirement home in the country – but a typical break in the St Hope's staffroom.

St Hope's excitable, greying Headmaster, Kenneth Flatley, looked around the room expectantly. His colleagues slumped further in their low staffroom chairs. But Mr Flatley knew the downbeat atmosphere was about to change. Just wait until they heard the news! He let the big grin on his face widen and made the announcement.

'The Prime Minister . . .' he said, feeling like he was about to burst with excitement, 'is coming to St Hope's *today*!'

Mr Flatley hung on to the last word and watched his staff . . . well, do nothing. It didn't looked like anything was going to alleviate their boredom today. Undeterred, Mr Flatley went on.

'He'll be presenting the annual Bravekidz Awards, for kids who've done something . . . . um . . . especially brave or kind.'

Still no reaction. Mr Flatley wrung his hands in frustration. Surely they would be excited when they found out what he had to say next? Ever the optimist, he continued his speech.

'The ceremony is being held here, because one of our pupils has . . . um . . .'

Still no reaction.

'Won the top prize!'

Mr Flatley wondered if the silence was that of sheer disbelief. But he just *knew* everyone would perk up once they got used to the idea and the Prime Minister arrived.

Working down in the bowels of the school at M.I. High's headquarters, Lenny had pulled quite a few strings to ensure the Bravekidz Awards took place at St Hope's School. But, for reasons known only to him, he'd chosen Fifty Pence as the overall winner. And Ms Templeman was given the unenviable task of telling him.

She found the wannabe rapper lurking suspiciously by a cupboard in the corridor.

'Who, me?' Fifty Pence babbled, his voice an octave higher than usual. 'A Bravekid?' The bravest thing he'd done recently was rescue a pound from a younger kid's wallet.

Forgetting the reason why he'd been hanging around the hallway, Fifty Pence swaggered off, feeling as if he had won a Brit Award. The moment he was gone, the cupboard door creaked open and three sets of wide eyes appeared.

'Quick! He's gone. Let's go – quick, quick!' a small voice urged.

Three Juniors tumbled out of the cupboard. They were grateful to have escaped such a close call with the school bully and still have their lunch-money intact. The three fled for their lives in the opposite direction, far away from where Fifty Pence had gone.

The Guinea Pig watched the Grand Master stroking the white rabbit perched on his lap. He looked powerful today – his expensive scarlet dressing down with gold lapels could clearly be seen, even as he sat amid a pool of shadows. He was addressing her via a monitor in her secret lab.

'Congratulations on your work, Guinea Pig,' he said, the letters 'S.K.U.L' appearing along the bottom of the screen. 'General Flopsy and I are impressed. Aren't we, Flopsy?'

The white rabbit blinked up at him.

'But the Super-Kriminal Underworld League spon-sored your research and now you must help us.'

The Guinea Pig smiled an evil grin. 'Grand Master

– relax!' she replied confidently. 'My scientific trials are complete. The world is about to see what we are capable of!'

And with this she let out a grotesque cackle that resonated around the science lab. The Guinea Pig was filled with glee. She and S.K.U.L were *finally* going to take over the world!

'Your mission is to investigate the Prime Minister,' instructed Lenny.

The three teenage spies, standing together in the M.I. High headquarters, looked at each other hopefully.

'Daisy, you'll go undercover as a reporter for the *United Schools Gazette*,' Lenny continued. 'Find out why he's behaving so aggressively.'

Daisy pulled a smug grin. She loved the idea of having a juicy character role to play for her first assignment.

'We need a suspect profile – personal history, family background . . .' Rose added. 'Plus we'll need blood and DNA samples.'

Blane looked puzzled. What on earth was DNA?

Rose could see he didn't have a clue. 'Deoxyribonucleic acid,' she sighed. 'Life's building block.'

'Yeah,' Daisy chimed in, even though she hadn't known either.

Blane scowled at Daisy. They were never friends in school, so why should they get along now? Besides, what did she have to offer the team but her talent for being a drama queen?

'How are you going to go undercover with such a big mouth?' he demanded.

'At least I'm not hired muscle.' Daisy shot back.

'You mean *martial arts expert*,' Blane corrected. 'Which beats being an expert in make-up!'

Rose had had enough. If she didn't stop these two squabbling they'd never get *anything* done.

'Guys – who knows why M.I.9 chose us,' she cut in, 'but we're in this together. It's our first mission – we can't afford to mess it up.'

Lenny, who'd been watching the argument unfold with amusement, stepped in to explain why each agent had been selected. As he confirmed Rose had been chosen for her scientific genius, Daisy for her ability to be a social chameleon and Blane for his expertise in martial arts, Lenny started to feel a bit nostalgic. He began to think of his early days in the secret service.

'I remember my first mission,' he said dreamily. 'Brighton Beach, crack of dawn, rubber dinghy . . .'

The three teen spies looked at each other impatiently. Forget fighting with each other – Lenny's reminiscing would keep them here all day.

'Gadgets, Lenny?' Blane interrupted.

'Oh yes,' their mentor blinked, snapping back to reality. 'Sorry.'

First, Lenny produced an ordinary-looking notepad.

'A DNA analyser,' he explained, flipping open the cover to reveal a series of pads and lights.

The next device was a deceptively harmless small silver tube.

'And this is a Lipstick Laser – it can cut a hole in metal at ten metres.'

Lipstick? Daisy seemed pretty pleased, but Blane was furious. What was with all these girly gadgets?

'Come on, Blane,' Daisy grinned, pulling off the lid and aiming the tube straight at him. 'Pucker up!'

A split second later, a red laser beam shot out from the tube, ricocheting off the walls and missing Blane by centimetres. Sparks flew around the room.

Daisy struggled to keep the tube under control, but it was no good. Another laser bolt shot out. Blane – quite sure he didn't want to be frazzled by a lipstick – sprang out of the way and back-flipped across the room, landing in a casual kung-fu stance.

Daisy's face burned red with embarrassment as she looked down at her smouldering lipstick. Frying Blane wouldn't look good on her M.I.9 record.

'You might want to keep a lid on that, Daisy,' Lenny suggested sarcastically, quickly moving on. 'Now, it's vital you memorize the details of the reporter legend we've created for you.'

Lenny passed Daisy a red box. While she was busy examining the contents, he continued explaining her role.

'Your name is Charlotte Graham,' he said. 'Remember, any deviation from the facts will compromise the mission and could put you in deadly danger.'

But Daisy was only half listening. She'd already switched to super-sleuth reporter mode. She held up the lipstick tube, pretending it was a microphone.

'Hi,' she simpered. 'This is Charlotte Graham. Pleasure to meet you, Prime Minister. My hair? Oh, it's, um, just something casual.'

Rose giggled, but Blane wasn't interested in Daisy's theatrics. In fact, he was getting frustrated.

'What's my role in all of this?' he demanded. It better be something good – after all, he'd got top marks in target practice last week!

'You'll be covering Daisy,' Lenny replied, while Blane stared at him blankly. 'Just hide in plain sight and act as a counter surveillance.'

'Um, it's another word for backup,' smirked Daisy, feeling superior. 'As in, you'll be backup for *me*!'

'Great!' Blane winced, his heart sinking. 'They get to save the world, and all I do is watch?'

Blane felt sick. Working with Daisy was annoying enough, but being her *backup* while she got to be involved in all the action? It wasn't only insulting – it was totally unfair!

# Chapter 5

It-girls Daisy, Kaleigh and Zara strode confidently through the school, trailed closely by Rose. Every now and then Kaleigh and Zara would turn round and shoot Rose a disdainful glare – if only they knew why the class nerd was following them!

Of course, Daisy knew she and Rose had to keep together for the mission, but neither of them would dream of being nice to each other in the schoolyard at St Hope's.

'Can you believe people are copying us already?' Daisy grinned to her two friends. She wasn't able to decide whether or not she liked the fact that Kaleigh, Zara and at least three other girls had already swept their hair up into the same hairdo she'd adopted only this morning. At least it proved that she was still St Hope School's number-one trendsetter.

'Didn't you copy your hairstyle from the actress on telly?' Rose piped up.

'And *who* are you, again?' Zara sneered, waving at Rose dismissively.

'She just doesn't get fashion, does she?' Kaleigh sniggered.

But Rose wasn't going to give up that easily. She hurried after them.

'Why worry about something that only lasts a moment?' she said. She wished they would see just how shallow they were being.

The girls looked at Rose like she was one of the sea cucumbers Ms Templeman had been droning on about in class this morning.

'Loser!' spat Kaleigh, as they quickened their pace. They had better things to do than be followed by this weirdo all day – Rose could be such a geek!


'You know how I told you about the aliens cloning the army? Well, I think I've intercepted some of their signals!'

Blane cast his friend a sideways glance, un-impressed. Stewart was still pestering him to come to his radio club at lunchtime, although Blane had already said he couldn't make it. And now he was telling him he'd discovered a transmission from outer space! Blane sighed. It was hard enough keeping his secret life as an M.I.9 agent from the rest of the school, let alone his best friend. Stewart's life *revolved* around uncovering unexplained theories.

'This is huge!' Stewart insisted urgently. 'What's got into you these days? You've got more secrets than the CIA.'

Blane's back stiffened. Was Stewart on to him?

'Look,' Stewart added, noticing Blane's sudden awkwardness. 'We've been mates since we were six. I can tell when you're lying.'

Blane took a deep breath and motioned Stewart closer to the lockers they were standing beside in the corridor. Glancing over his shoulder to check no one was around, he lowered his voice and looked at Stewart solemnly.

'Look, Stew . . . I think there's something you should know.'

Stewart nodded eagerly, sensing his mate was about to let him in on some seriously big secret. Maybe Blane knew more about the aliens than he'd been letting on.

'But you must swear not to tell anyone . . .'

Before Blane could say another word, a locker door slammed painfully into the back of his head.

'Ow!' he yelled spinning round. Daisy was right in front of him, tapping her foot.

'Telling tales?' she asked accusingly.

'Butt out, bimbo!' Blane growled. Curses! He couldn't tell Stewart now – besides, who did Cosmetic Queen think she was?

A huge banner declaring 'WELCOME, PRIME MINISTER!' was flapping in the wind above a flurry of activity in the St Hope's quadrangle. A TV crew were setting up equipment in a corner. Mr Flatley was busy gushing to Ms Templeman about what a great day it was going to be.

'Let's hope it all goes to plan,' he babbled, elated. The Headmaster was determined this visit would finally put St Hope's firmly on the map. But they had to go through a checklist first.

'We've excluded the worst troublemakers . . .' promised Ms Templeman, following up Mr Flatley's request to make sure the visit wouldn't be interrupted by unruly students. 'Well, two hundred of them, anyway.'

'Good, good,' nodded Mr Flatley, 'Um, what about the staff?'

'I've told some of them to go home too . . .'

'Right – good idea,' he nodded happily. Everything was going according to plan, and Britain's Prime Minister would be at St Hope's any minute.

Rose and Blane were watching the proceedings from the other side of the schoolyard.

'Were you really going to tell Stewart about our mission?' asked Rose anxiously.

Blane rolled his eyes. On top of having to be her backup AND smashing him in the head with the locker door, Daisy had dobbed him in too.

'No way,' Blane said, pretending not to care. 'Daisy doesn't know what she's talking about.'

'This is serious,' Rose pressed, looking grave. Didn't Blane realize M.I.9 would close them down if their identities were exposed?

Before Blane could reply, they spotted a reporter stepping purposefully across the quadrangle. With her short black bob, large glasses and neat black suit, it took Rose and Blane a minute to realize that this was Agent Daisy Millar in full character. She was carrying the DNA-analyser notepad.

'She's good, isn't she?' said Rose, noticing Blane's grudging admiration. She was about to head back down to M.I. High HQ, but wouldn't have missed Daisy's amazing transformation for the world.

Their observation was interrupted by an excited squeal coming from the other side of the schoolyard. Mr Flatley was becoming hysterical.

'The Prime Minister – he's here!'

Right on cue, a group of bodyguards in black suits swarmed into the yard, followed by the PM. He surveyed the scene with a steely gaze.

Mr Flatley burst out of the gaggle of onlookers, followed closely by Daisy.

'Welcome to St Hope's, Prime Minister!' he beamed, breathlessly. 'I'm Kenneth Flatley, Headmaster. And this is Charlotte Graham, a reporter from the *United Schools Gazette*.'

Daisy reached for the Prime Minister's hand as she smiled sweetly.

'Thank you for granting me an interview, Prime Minister.'

Daisy tried not to wince as he returned a bone-crunching shake. The Prime Minister looked around impatiently.

'Can we get this ceremony underway as soon as possible?' he scowled at Mr Flatley. 'I've an important announcement to make afterwards.'

Mr Flatley didn't notice the dark look in the Prime Minister's eyes. Instead, he was sure it meant the nation's leader had a surprise planned for the school. What a day for St Hope's!

'Yes,' added the PM abruptly. 'Our troops are mobilized and ready to strike across Europe. They only await my final instruction.'

Daisy's mouth fell open. Maybe this was the shocking plan they'd feared!

As she followed the Prime Minister and his entourage into the school hall, Daisy made an urgent call on her Pencil Communicator.

Already down in the headquarters, Rose received the transmission.

'This is getting serious!' Daisy whispered urgently. 'The PM is going to launch an attack on Europe!'

Taking only a moment to register the terrible news, Rose sprung into action and quickly contacted Blane. Was he in position?

Sitting behind a curtain on the hall stage, Blane flicked absentmindedly through the *Counter-Surveillance* textbook. Being a spy might have been his dream come true, but this was *so* boring. 'There's zero happening this end,' he reported. 'It's Dullsville.'

'Just don't let Daisy out of your sight!' Rose chided.

'Yeah, yeah,' Blane grumbled. For goodness' sake – it's not as if this part of the mission was important or anything. 'Counter-surveillance. I *can* do my job.'

On the other side of the hall, the PM headed for his dressing room, flanked by one of his bodyguards.

'Subject on the move,' whispered Daisy into her Pencil Communicator. 'Going to try for an interview – *and* some DNA.'

Back in one of St Hope's classrooms, Blane's best friend was having a far more interesting time. Crowded round a large old-style black transmitter he'd built at home, Stewart and the other sole member of the lunchtime radio club were listening intently to strange warbling noises coming from the speakers. Strapped awkwardly with elastic bands to the front of the radio was another one, coloured silver. The two were connected with purple leads.

'It's *definitely* an alien language,' Stewart said confidently, his voice breaking.

But as he twiddled a few knobs, the gravity of the situation hit him. He hadn't expected *this*.

'Whatever it is . . .' he whispered, his mouth dry, '*it's inside the school!*'

# Chapter 6

Blane peered out from behind the backstage curtain. How could he be so stupid? He'd been so busy telling Rose he had everything under control that he hadn't even bothered to keep an eye on Daisy. And now she – and the PM – was nowhere to be seen. So much for brushing up on his counter-surveillance skills. Where had they gone?

Daisy, meanwhile, had followed the PM and his bodyguard down the corridor. Right now, she was fluttering her eyelids and smiling sweetly at the bodyguard. But the rather beefy Don Ackminster was a fellow who liked to stick to instructions. He wasn't buying any of Daisy's charm.

'Sorry, love,' he replied gruffly, as the teen spy tried to talk her way into the PM's dressing room. 'This area is off-limits. Boss's orders.'

Even when Daisy told him she had an interview with the Prime Minister, Don refused to let her inside. She'd have to try another tack.

'Oh, Prime Minister?' Daisy cooed, looking into

the air behind the bodyguard. Just as she expected, Don turned to see if the PM really was emerging from his room. Daisy expertly dug her hand into the bodyguard's back and swiftly played out one of the moves she'd learned during the secret-agent training. Don's head immediately jerked backwards as he froze on the spot.

'Wow!' marvelled Daisy. 'The Mysake Five Finger Freeze works a treat!'

Stepping around the incapacitated bodyguard, Daisy twisted the doorknob. As she crept into the room, she could see the back of the PM, sitting in a chair. He didn't seem to be moving. This was getting weird.

'Hello?' she said, taking a few hesitant steps forward. 'Prime Minister?'

The PM didn't move a muscle.

'Rose!' hissed Daisy into her Pencil Communicator and peering over the top of the chair. 'I'm with the PM. He seems to be asleep!'

Rose was waiting for Daisy's call. She quickly told Daisy to get some samples.

'Any piece of skin or fingernail will do,' Rose urged.

'How about dandruff?' Daisy asked, surveying the multiple white flecks dotting the collar of the Prime Minister's suit jacket. As disgusting as it was, it might be the only solution.

'Perfect!'

'Gross!' Daisy took a swab stick out of the DNA

notepad and collected some of the dandruff flakes. 'Britain's PM needs to learn to rinse after he shampoos.'

Trying to ignore her own revulsion, Daisy placed the swab back in the notepad. Green lights flashed as the results transmitted back to Rose down in M.I. High HQ.

'OK, Prime Minister,' Rose said to herself. 'Let's see what makes you tick!'

Nothing could have prepared the teen spy for what came up on screen. Rose was horrified as an image of the PM's face appeared, spliced down the middle. One half seemed like that of a normal human being. But, somehow, the other half looked almost *robotic*.

'Daisy! It's the PM!' Rose blurted into the communicator. '*You have to get out of there!*'

Back in the dressing room, Daisy had just enough time to spin round to see the Prime Minister's eyes suddenly spring open. Standing up, he shot Daisy a menacing look.

'Um, I . . . I'm Charlotte Millar,' she spluttered, caught momentarily off-guard. 'Charlotte Graham. I mean Charlotte *Millar* Graham . . .'

With Rose shouting in her ear, Daisy was trying hard to concentrate. She had to get out of the room, and quickly.

'So . . .' she said, flashing him a hopeful grin. 'How do you feel about meeting Britain's bravest kids?'

The Prime Minister's eyes narrowed. Daisy could feel a chill creeping up her spine.

'Are *you* brave, Miss Millar?' he said.

'I . . . think so,' Daisy's voice quavered. The PM's icy glare was seriously freaking her out.

'Then let's stop wasting our time!' the PM thundered, snatching the notepad from Daisy's hand and ripping open the cover.

'DNA analysis – one of your special interests?' he snarled.

Daisy was beginning to feel more like a caged rabbit than an M.I. High agent. She desperately tried to ease the tension.

'Science is always popular with our readers!' she smiled, hoping she sounded convincing.

The PM just stared at her. There was something about the chilling look in his eyes. They just didn't seem *human*. Daisy felt a sudden wave of anger roll over her.

'Who *are* you?' she demanded.

That did it. The PM snorted and strode towards the door.

'Interview your way out of *this*!' he laughed over his shoulder, storming out of the room.

There was an unmistakable sound of a key turning in the lock as Daisy remained frozen to the spot. She was trapped!

After a tense minute, she sighed with relief as she remembered Blane was backing her up. *But shouldn't he be here by now?*

# Chapter 7

Blane was panicking now. Where on earth were Daisy and the PM? He flipped frantically through the *Counter-Surveillance* textbook.

'Losing subject,' he muttered anxiously to himself. 'Must be under L . . .'

Rose's voice coming through the Pencil Communicator broke his concentration. Blane tried to fob her off. He had more important things to worry about right now.

'It's Daisy!'

'What's she done now?' said Blane, suddenly annoyed. 'Broken a fingernail?'

'No . . .' Rose sounded anxious. 'She's in real trouble . . . as you'd know if you'd been doing your job!'

Blane's heart plummeted. He'd screwed up and he knew it. If he didn't leave the hall and find Daisy and the PM now, he might be thrown out of M.I.9 altogether. Without further thought, he jumped off the stage and bolted through the hall.

'No running, please, Blane!' he heard Ms Templeman call after him.

But Blane ignored her. He was an M.I.9 agent, and M.I.9 agents didn't stop for teachers' orders.

But there was another obstacle ahead. Stewart was blocking his path, waving his home-made radio.

'You won't believe this! You *have* to listen!'

Blane tried desperately to move around his friend, but Stewart just plunked his tall frame in front of him again. He might have been Blane's best mate, but sometimes his timing was as bad as his dorky haircut!

'I'm picking up alien signals,' he whispered urgently, eyes wide. 'From *inside the school.*'

Blane managed to side-step Stewart this time, and took off down the corridor, desperate to lose him. But Stewart matched him stride for stride.

'Oh, it'll be that taxi company in North Wales again,' Blane replied casually. 'Remember . . . you thought they were Martians?'

'Not this time,' insisted Stewart. 'The signal's centred on Westminster. It moved east until it got here.'

*Huh*? Blane stopped abruptly. 'Westminster?' he repeated. 'As in the *Houses of Parliament* Westminster?'

'Yeah,' Stewart nodded. He was pleased to see Blane finally interested; maybe he could get him to come to the radio club now. 'And it's transmitting from really close by.'

To Stewart's surprise, Blane made a sudden grab for the radio.

'I need to borrow this,' he said. By the serious look

on his face, Stewart was sure it wasn't a request. 'I'll
explain later.'

'Look after it,' Stewart shouted, as Blane sprinted
off. 'Are you sure you don't want me to come?'

Stewart watched in dismay as the figure of his best
friend disappeared down the corridor. He just couldn't
figure out why Blane had been behaving so strangely
over the last few days.


Still trapped in the dressing room, Daisy was beginning
to stress out. She *had* to get back to the hall before
the Prime Minister declared World War Three.

Daisy tried the door handle, but it wouldn't budge.
She listened against the door. There was nothing to
be heard – not even the heavy breathing of Don the
security guard!

*Think, Daisy, think . . .* she coaxed herself. *That's it!
The Lipstick Laser!*

Daisy grabbed the silver tube from her bag and
carefully twisted off the lid. She hoped she could
hold it still enough. She really didn't want a repeat of
that morning's performance when she nearly zapped
Blane. Daisy closed her eyes and pointed the Lipstick
Laser at the door.

Nothing happened.

Daisy cautiously opened her eyes to check she'd
taken the lid off properly. But, as it turned out, the tube
she was holding wasn't the Lipstick Laser. It was just
a normal lipstick tube. Daisy breathed a sigh of relief.

Still, the colour really was fantastic, and how could a girl go on and save the world if she wasn't looking good? Daisy applied a quick top-up of colour to her lips before reaching for the real M.I.9 Lipstick Laser that Lenny had given her. She tried again.

Sure enough, this time a red beam of light shot out. The laser swiftly created a small ball of flame and easily cut through the wood. Within seconds the door burst outwards and landed with a thud on the floor outside, in a massive cloud of swirling smoke.

Daisy emerged spluttering from the debris to find a young St Hope's kid standing frozen in the hallway, unable to believe what he'd just seen.

Coughing, Daisy frantically fanned the haze away.

'See,' she told the wide-eyed kid sternly, 'smoking really *is* bad for you!'

Back in the hall, a group of children and one very proud Mr Flatley were standing on stage beside the Prime Minister, ready to begin the Bravekidz Awards. As the overall winner of the competition, Fifty Pence was standing at the far end of the queue. He would be the last to receive his Bravekidz rosette from the PM. Fifty Pence shifted his feet from side to side – he was still trying to figure out just what he had done to earn such an honour.

Further up the line, a posh kid called Giles Tomkins from a nearby school was stealing a bitter glance at Fifty Pence, while his friend scowled beside him. 'I should have walked this,' he muttered, snidely. Mummy says the results were a fix.'

'Well done, Giles!' a glowing Mr Flatley interrupted. 'You saved a rambler from a flock of crazed sheep, using only a stunt knife and an electric cattle prod!'

Giles walked forward glumly to let the PM pin the large blue rosette on his jumper.

Free of her school-room prison, Daisy finally made her way back to M.I. High HQ. She was not at all happy.

'Daisy!' Rose cried, running up to greet her as she stormed out of the lift. 'Thank goodness you're safe!'

'No thanks to *Mr Surveillance*,' Daisy spat, scowling at Blane who had returned sometime earlier.

'I'm here now, aren't I?' snapped Blane.

'Look, can we sort this out later?' Rose said, cutting them off. She wasn't keen for a repeat of the row they'd had earlier. 'The Prime Minister is a cyber-clone!'

Blane looked at her blankly.

'Half-man, half-machine,' Rose explained. 'The DNA tests confirmed it, but I can't work out how he's being operated. It could be software . . . or voice activation . . . or even radio waves.'

Blane's eyes lit up. *For once, there might just be something in Stewart's crackpot theories!*

'That would explain this!' He held up the home-made radio. 'Stewart's been picking up weird signals.'

Rose could hardly contain her delight.

'This is great!' she said. 'If we can follow this back to

its source, then we can find out who's controlling the Prime Minister.'

This time, both of her fellow agents looked confused.

'It's using a phase shift PSK31 mode,' Rose quickly explained. 'On a 31.25 kilohertz band. It means it's nearby – oh, I'll go!

'But what about the robo-clone Prime Minister thing?' asked Daisy. 'He's going to declare war any minute now!'

'Leave him to me,' announced Blane. Daisy stared at him pityingly.

'Backup boy wonder?' she laughed. 'I don't think so!'

Blane sighed wearily. He knew he was going to have to apologize eventually, so it might as well get it over with.

'Look, I messed up and I was wrong about you pulling off the reporter thing,' he said begrudgingly. 'But trust me. I *can* do this!'

Seeing the earnest expression on Blane's face was enough to make Daisy give in. After all, they *did* have World War Three to try and stop today.

'OK. We'll *both* go,' she decided. 'But you'd better not mess up this time!'

# Chapter 8

Behind the hall's stage, Daisy and Blane crouched down in the wings. As Mr Flatley droned on about how amazing the Bravekidz Award ceremony had been for St Hope's, Daisy peered sullenly out at the audience.

'I don't believe this!' she whispered furiously, trying to count how many of the girls had now adopted her new hairstyle. 'I wanted to stand out from the crowd!

Blane shook his head. Typical Daisy!

'Focus, Daisy!' he ordered.

They *had* to stop the PM from making the announcement, and Blane had an idea. Within seconds he'd pulled the rope that closed the stage curtains and had his hand pressed firmly against a fire alarm on the wall.

There was instant mayhem.

Screams and shouts filled the hall as students and teachers scrambled for the exit. Mr Flatley, his head dizzy with the prospect that this incredible day for St Hope's could come to such a spectacularly chaotic end, was knocked to the ground in the panic.

Backstage, Blane and the Prime Minister had already come face-to-face. Daisy might have turned Don into a stupefied waxwork with another Mysake Five Finger Freeze for the second time today, but it certainly hadn't put the PM out of action.

The PM looked around wildly and then pulled on a stage rope hanging from the ceiling. A sandbag came smashing towards the ground, heading straight for Blane.

He leapt out of the way and the sandbag crashed to the floor. He had just narrowly escaped being crushed to a pulp!

The PM grabbed Blane with his right hand and dragged him to his feet.

'You cannot stop us now!' he snarled. 'My next announcement will be a declaration of war!'

But Blane wasn't about to give up that easily. In one swift move, he tightly held the Prime Minister's arm and threw him to the floor.

Blane watched as the PM's head twitched several times. His mind spun as he realized something else just wasn't quite right.

*Where was the man's hand?*

Except for a few red and white wires dangling from the empty hole, there was nothing at the end of the right arm of the PM's suit jacket.

With disgust, Blane realized that he was still clutching the severed hand of the Prime Minister. But that was nothing – the hand was suddenly coming to life!

Blane tried to shake it off, but the dismembered body-part had an iron grip. And, what was worse, it seemed to have a mind of its own!

On the other side of the curtain, things were starting to calm down. The fire alarm had stopped and teachers were slowly leading pupils back into the hall.

Mr Flatley struggled to his feet, grabbing the podium to steady himself.

'What happened, Charlotte?' he asked, dazed, as the still-disguised Daisy appeared by his side.

'Oh, just a faulty fire alarm,' smiled the charming reporter, taking his arm.

Mr Flatley nodded. 'Oh, right.'

'We'll soon get things back to normal,' she assured him.

*CRASH!*

'AAAAHHHH!'

*What was Blane up to back there?* Daisy needed to try to cover up the banging and yelling coming from backstage. There would be nothing worse than Mr Flatley going to investigate and discovering one of his students battling it out with a cyber-clone.

'So! While we're waiting . . .' Daisy announced loudly, fixing her eyes on the audience and improvising like mad. 'I suggest we find out a little bit more about the fascinating man standing next to me. Where exactly did the Flatley story begin?'

Daisy turned expectantly to St Hope's Headmaster,

Rose was a scientific genius and loved nothing
more than solving complex problems.

'The world is about to see what we are capable of!'
the Guinea Pig cackled.

This was it – their very first mission!

'I have an important announcement to make,' the Prime Minister declared.

'Thank you for granting me this interview,
Prime Minister,' Daisy said sweetly.

The radio signal led Rose to the Guinea Pig's secret laboratory.

The Prime Minister is a cyber-clone!

Blane couldn't let Stewart find out about his secret spy work.

Kaleigh and Zara loved Crush almost as much as Daisy did.

Fifty Pence and his posse saw boy-band Crush
as a great business opportunity.

As Crush played on, the hall became a heaving mass of zombies.

Rose couldn't believe it – she was rocking the house with her song!

Thanks to spies extraordinaire Daisy, Blane and Rose, Britain was safe once more.

who, in turn, looked relieved that everything was running smoothly again. Trying to ignore Blane's shouts coming from behind her, she just hoped Rose would think of a plan, quick-smart!

# Chapter 9

With all the commotion going on in the hall, no one noticed Rose slip out the school gates, clutching Stewart's makeshift radio. As she monitored the radio signals, she noticed they were getting stronger with every step she took. The transmission must be close by.

Dashing down the street, Rose held the radio out in front of her. She came to a stop outside a large run-down warehouse as the signal went crazy. This had to be it! Checking around to make sure she wasn't being followed, Rose stepped inside.

She was surprised to find that the signal led her to the entrance of a dimly-lit laboratory. Among the dishevelled clutter of half-constructed equipment and oddly-deformed mannequins, Rose could see the back of a person dressed in a white lab coat, wearing a bizarre helmet with dozens of wires poking out of the top.

The figure was playing what looked like some sort of crazy computer game. Only, it wasn't a game – on the screen in front, Rose could clearly see the severed hand of the fake Prime Minister attacking Blane in the hall.

'Oh, stupid boy!' the figure was cackling, urging the hand on. 'My cyber-clone has the strength of ten men!'

'It's even worse than I thought!' Rose gasped aloud. She cursed her stupidity – *why couldn't she keep her mouth shut, just once?*

The scientist spun round. 'This is a science laboratory!' she shouted, pointing an accusing finger at Rose. 'And *you* are trespassing!'

Rose winced in horror. For the second time that day, she realized she was looking at something that *just wasn't quite human*. A white-whiskered snout protruded from under the helmet.

'This isn't science,' Rose snapped furiously, quickly regaining her composure. 'It's playing God!'

She could almost *feel* the being's eyes under the helmet, looking at her with disdain.

'*That's* where you're wrong!' she yelled, turning back towards the screen. 'DESTROY!'

Rose watched in disbelief as the hand moved in and repeatedly zeroed in on Blane. He continued to kick at it furiously, but the hand kept up its frenzied attack – this time aiming for his throat. Even Rose could see he wouldn't be able to hold it off for much longer.

'Let him go!' she cried.

But whatever this creature controlling the madness in front of her was, it had obviously already made plans for Blane – and it had other plans in mind for Rose, too. With a single command of 'Seize her!', an arm from a headless mannequin shot out and grabbed the teenage spy, followed quickly by several more.

Rose couldn't move. And, worse still, she realized she'd dropped Stewart's radio.

The scientist quietly moved closer to Rose and finally lifted off her helmet. What emerged from beneath it were the unmistakable features of a guinea pig – quivering whiskers twitched curiously, while a large pair of glasses rested on a white furry snout. This creature was clearly the result of a cloning experiment gone terribly wrong.

If Rose wasn't being held so tightly, she would have looked away from the hideous sight. But as the rodent stepped closer, a tremor of recognition rippled across Rose's face.

'Professor Sally Moreau!' she gasped.

'You know me?' asked the professor, secretly impressed. Her fame had spread further than she had ever imagined.

'Any scientist worth their sodium chloride knows of you and your discredited experiments!' said Rose contemptuously.

'If you're a scientist then you should be on the side of progress!' Professor Moreau snapped back.

Rose was *really* angry now. 'This isn't progress, this is madness!' she yelled. 'Look at you!'

Rose knew she wasn't ever going to be able to

reason with this lunatic. But if only she could get hold of Stewart's radio . . .

Harnessing all her strength, Rose heaved her shoulders, shrugging herself free from the arms that encircled her. Before the Guinea Pig had time to react, Rose snatched Stewart's radio up off the floor and held it out, so that its speakers were directly facing the professor.

Compared to the sickening confidence she'd been displaying just moments before, the scientist looked suddenly panicked.

'Something bothering you, rodent features?' demanded Rose. She knew that guinea pigs were susceptible to high-frequency sound waves. And judging by the expression on Moreau's face, *she* knew it as well.

'You wouldn't dare!' Moreau screeched hoarsely.

*Oh, yes I would!* Rose said to herself, advancing towards the shrieking creature and cranking up the transmitter. Professor Moreau tried vainly to cover her deformed ears.

All Rose needed to do was give the dial one . . . final . . . *twist*.

The Guinea Pig screamed in agony, crashing unconscious into a heap on the floor.

Without a moment to lose, Rose threw down the radio and grabbed the helmet Moreau had been wearing. From what she'd seen when she walked into the lab, she was sure this was how the crazed scientist had been controlling the cyber-clone Prime Minister.

'Hang on, Blane,' Rose shouted at the screen, frantically pulling out her Pencil Communicator. 'I've just got to try to work this thing out!'

# Chapter 10

Blane was relieved to hear Rose's voice crackling through the Pencil Communicator.

*SMACK!* He punched the severed hand away.

Only moments before . . .

*SMASH!*

. . . he'd tried to contact both Rose *and* Daisy . . .

*CRASH!*

. . . but neither had got back to him until now. He was beginning to think they had forgotten all about him.

*THUMP!*

*But where were they?* He wished his team would hurry up. His relentless foe showed no signs of tiring and continued to lunge and claw at him. No matter how many times he punched the severed hand or kicked it away, or threw it against the wall, it just kept coming back for more.

It didn't help that he could hear Daisy in front of the curtain, bravely plugging on with her Mr Flatley interview.

'And so . . . having caravanning as a hobby helps

you to switch off from such a high-pressure job?' he heard her ask, pretending to be fascinated.

*She doesn't know the last thing about high-pressure!* he thought, fighting off the disembodied hand as it launched at him yet again. But Blane was too busy fending it off to notice the PM cyber-clone on the floor – it had started to quiver and twitch into life.

Blane desperately looked around for another avenue of attack. Out of the corner of his eye, he could see a rope dangling from the ceiling – right next to the one the PM had pulled while trying to crush Blane before. It was now or never.

Just as the hand prepared to hurtle towards his throat one more time, Blane quickly reached out and yanked the rope. A heavy sandbag plummeted with alarming speed, crashing down on the hand and pinning it to the ground. It gave a final shudder and then lay still.

'Not so handy now!' Blane snorted. A wave of relief washed over him. If he hadn't mashed the hand first, the hand certainly would have mashed him.

Blane hardly had time to reflect on his victory though, because without warning, the cyber-clone Prime Minister stood up and marched right past him. Blane could only watch helplessly as the PM parted the curtains and exited the backstage area. Frantic, he whispered into his Pencil Communicator.

'Rose! *Hurry up!*'

\* \* \*

Stewart Critchley had had enough of listening to Charlotte Graham's boring interview with Mr Flatley. He'd been trying to sit in the audience very patiently since the drama with the fire alarm, but he was starting to smell a rat.

'Something weird is going on!' he muttered to himself. 'I'm gonna get my radio back. Those alien clones have got to be *somewhere* close.'

Stewart made his way backstage, just in time to see Blane shoving a pencil into his pocket as he appeared at the foot of the stairs.

'Hey, what's going on?' he demanded.

'I was just helping with the fire alarm,' lied Blane, feeling uncomfortable.

'That's no fire alarm,' insisted Stewart. 'It's the alien task force! I need my radio *now*, quick!'

'I put it back in your locker,' Blane freewheeled, feeling guilty about once again lying to his best friend. 'It's still picking up some *amazing* stuff.'

'I knew it! They've landed! They've landed!' Stewart squealed. He was halfway out the door already. 'Are you coming?'

'Um, I'll catch up with you,' called Blane. He had to find out where the PM had got to.

Blane walked out into the hall to find Mr Flatley's dreary life story still unfolding.

'Freshwater fish are, of course, easier to keep . . .' he droned – just as the Prime Minister's head suddenly popped through the curtains.

'Oh, uh . . . the Prime Minister's back,' cut in Daisy, spinning round.

She quickly placed the microphone on its stand and edged away, leaving the Headmaster and PM together.

Blane was waiting for her at the side of the stage.

'Has Rose got control of him yet?' whispered Daisy urgently.

Blane looked worried. 'I dunno. I lost radio contact!'

Daisy reached into her pocket and pulled out the Lipstick Laser.

'Taking out the TV cameras will totally blow our cover,' she said anxiously. 'But it might be the only way.'

'No!' Blane held up his hand, indicating they had to wait. 'We have to give Rose a chance.'

# Chapter 11

Back in Professor Moreau's lab, Rose was putting on the mind-control helmet.

A confusion of pictures and words flashed up in front of her. But as Rose finally registered what she was looking at, her heart soared.

She was seeing exactly what the cyber-clone Prime Minister was! This was how Professor Moreau controlled him.

Rose found herself looking out at the audience in the assembly hall, watching as the words 'PM CAM' flashed in front of her eyes.

'OK, so how does this thing work?' she muttered to herself.

Rose gulped as the PM clone in the school hall spoke up, echoing her words. 'So how does this thing work?'

'Whatever I think, the PM says . . .'

'The PM says,' garbled the PM clone, repeating Rose's words again. 'Er, no . . . er . . . what I meant to say was . . .'

She willed herself to concentrate. This could finally be her big chance to have her say, using the PM as her mouthpiece. Rose took a deep breath and allowed herself a quick smile. She was going to enjoy this!

'Listen in science classes and be res–' she began.

'–pectful to people who are good at it,' continued the PM clone in the hall. 'Er . . . now . . . er . . . I said I was going to make an important announcement and here it is . . .'

Still watching from the side of the stage, Daisy and Blane were worried. The future of the world would depend on the PM's next sentence. If Rose failed, World War Three could kick off immediately.

Daisy began to lift the Lipstick Laser, just in case. But Blane grabbed her hand and lowered it. He shook his head. They should wait and see what the PM said first.

The Prime Minister cleared his throat.

'I'm here today to talk of peace,' the PM assured his audience. 'Whatever our differences with the rest of Europe, we can work it out. People have just got to . . . *chill out*.'

There were smiles and nods of agreement from the attentive students. Mr Flatley was impressed. Here was a man who clearly knew how to speak to teenagers, and on their wavelength.

'Britain can be great again,' went on the PM, 'but only by listening to others and doing the right thing.'

'And, er . . .' the Prime Minister seemed to have

had a last-minute thought. Daisy and Blane held their breath.

'Science is cool!' the PM added enthusiastically.

Mr Flatley scratched his head and blinked, just as the Prime Minister's head appeared to jerk several times and drop forward. He looked as if he'd just fallen into a deep sleep.

The Headmaster did a double take, but decided the PM was just taking a bow. Mr Flatley puffed his chest out with pride and started to clap. It *was* a great day for St Hope's.

As the audience joined in wholeheartedly, cheering and whistling, the Headmaster moved over to the PM and tapped him on the shoulder. The Prime Minister remained absolutely still. Mr Flatley tried tapping him again. Perhaps the poor man was just exhausted – the Bravekidz Awards certainly hadn't turned out to be as straightforward as they'd expected.


Rose removed the helmet from her head, relieved that it was finally over. At least everyone might pay attention in Ms Templeman's science class from now on.

'Hello?'

Rose tensed. She could hear a trembling voice coming from a packing crate on the floor. But what if it was another one of Professor Moreau's grotesque dummy experiments?

'Hello? Oh dear . . . is anybody there?'

Rose grabbed the corner of the crate's lid and lifted

it up. She'd seen a lot of weird things today, but Rose could hardly believe her eyes when she saw who it was.

*The REAL British Prime Minister!*

The PM was crouching beneath some straw. He blinked up at her.

'Prime Minister!' gasped Rose. 'Don't worry – you're safe now.'

But the PM didn't seem to care about *that*. He had a more pressing concern.

'Do you know where the gentlemen's toilet is?' he asked urgently. 'I've been in here rather a long time!'

# Chapter 12

A short while later, Rose, Daisy and Blane emerged from the lift and strode proudly into M.I. High HQ. They'd just averted a major catastrophe – their first mission had been a success!

Lenny was already there waiting for them, standing beside the cyber-clone PM.

'Well, at least he's armless now!' he quipped, before bursting into laughter at his own joke.

The three secret agents stopped short in front of him, but didn't smile. Lenny's humour was not to be encouraged.

Lenny saw their impassive faces and abruptly stopped chuckling.

Rose reached over and pulled down the back of the cyber-clone's collar. A black cranium and the letters 'S.K.U.L.' were clearly stamped on the neck.

'The Guinea Pig's plan had "S.K.U.L." stamped all over it,' she observed wryly.

'Yes,' Lenny sighed. 'The Grand Master will use any disaffected party to try and cause chaos.'

The agents knew this wasn't the last they'd hear of the Grand Master and his cronies.

'The Guinea Pig's been arrested,' Daisy added, remembering to give Lenny one final update from their first mission. 'And we've sealed her lab for further investigation.'

Finally, it was time to relax. Britain was back on a peaceful path!

There was, however, at least one person *not* happy with the news that World War Three wasn't going to happen after all.

The Grand Master was sitting in his darkened lair, watching the evening's headline news in disbelief. His top lip quivered angrily as the words 'WAR CANCELLED, PEACE RESTORED' flashed up on the television. Footage of Mr Flatley standing next to the Prime Minister on the stage at St Hope's filled the screen.

The Grand Master's hand tensed as he stroked the giant white rabbit on his lap. *How had it all gone so horribly wrong?*

'Why isn't Britain at war?' he cried angrily, cradling his pet. 'Oh, you were right all along, Flopsy . . . never trust a guinea pig!'

Back at St Hope's School, Daisy and Rose stood in the hallway, watching as loads of girls wandered past sporting copy-cat styles of Daisy's hairdo.

'Poor Prime Minister,' Daisy sighed. 'I know how he feels. It's no fun having clones of yourself everywhere. You're lucky, Rose. No one ever copies you. You just do your own thing.'

Rose shrugged. 'I guess that's my style,' she replied.

'Yeah,' agreed Daisy, eyeing Rose's feet with a withering look that only a true fashionista could give. 'But you *really* should do something about those *shoes*!'

The girls' conversation was interrupted by a commotion erupting further down the corridor. Stewart's lanky frame was towering over Blane, holding the battered home-made radio up in fury.

'I really thought I put it back in your locker,' they heard Blane say, apologizing sheepishly. 'I must have dropped it during the fire drill.'

Stewart looked like he wasn't sure whether or not to believe him. He shot Blane a hurt look and stormed off.

'Poor Blane,' muttered Rose. 'He and Stewart were always so close.'

'Well, he's got us now. He'll work it out.' Daisy smiled chirpily, as Blane headed towards them. It was time for their debriefing with Lenny.

Lenny wasn't exactly big on praise, but the teen spies could tell he'd definitely been pleased with the outcome of their first ever M.I.9 assignment.

'Not bad for a first mission?' grinned Rose, as the

three pretended to bump into each other afterwards in the schoolyard.

Blane and Daisy smiled back at her. She was right – it was actually incredible once they thought about it. A few months ago they'd just been three very normal – and *very* different – schoolkids going about their day-to-day lives.

Now they were highly trained secret agents, working as a team to defeat S.K.U.L. and learning to appreciate each other for who they were. Even if some members did need help with jazzing up their school uniform a bit, Daisy noted, eyeing Rose's super-strict dress sense wearily.

'We've taken out an impostor PM and Britain's none the wiser,' added Blane, as if it was the most normal thing in the world.

But something was still bugging Daisy. 'But we're not even going to be famous,' she moaned, genuinely gutted.

'That's just as well,' laughed Rose, checking her watch. 'Cos we've got double science in five minutes!'

The three teenagers hitched up their bags and started towards class. But if any of them thought it was time to head back to normality, they were wrong. Right on cue, a small vibration starting buzzing in each of their pockets. As Daisy, Rose and Blane pulled out their Pencil Communicators, they smiled as they saw the ends of each secret-agent device flashing red.

It was going to be a busy day . . .

# Eyes on Their Stars

# M.I.HIGH

# **Chapter 1**

Inside a record store, somewhere in the Midlands, a tough-looking metal freak in a battered biker's jacket was nodding his head enthusiastically. With a pair of headphones clamped over his ears, he was enjoying the CD he'd picked at the store's listening station. The man's long bushy beard swayed perfectly in time with his silver nose ring.

*Nice.* Death metal was rocking his world.

The biker's perfect afternoon wasn't about to last much longer, though. Without warning, five young hoodies rampaged into the store and promptly got to work ripping CDs off the racks and knocking displays over. A deafening, high-pitched squeal filled the building as the biker yanked off his headphones. He'd seen plenty of menacing people in his time, but these kids just *didn't look quite right* . . .

All of them bore the same glazed look in their eyes, as though they weren't really registering the chaos they were causing. And they all had their arms outstretched in front of them, like they were teen zombies.

Whatever they were, the biker quickly decided

he'd rather not find out. No matter how much he was enjoying that new death-metal CD, he wasn't going to risk sticking around to buy it today.

He hurriedly detached himself from the listening station, picked up his backpack and fled terrified from the shop.

Tony Frisco was smugly watching the mayhem at the record store unfold.

Frisco was a music-industry mogul who had convinced himself he was cool and 'down with the kids'. But his white jacket and loud striped shirt told a different story. The truth was, with his shiny bald head perspiring as he watched the events unfold, Tony Frisco was about as cool as someone wearing woolly gloves in the Sahara.

The mogul was ensconced in a zebra-print chair in the middle of his busy Boogie Corp office. Staff worked around him diligently, their ears pressed against telephones. Frisco's eyes remained glued greedily to a giant plasma screen in front of him, as it relayed the anarchy in the record store.

'If music be the food of love,' cried Frisco, gazing at the screen with a mixture of glee and satisfaction, 'then play on, my zombie friends – PLAY ON!'

He clasped his hands excitedly and stood up. His plan was taking shape beautifully. Frisco could feel the adrenalin coursing through his veins.

'No one can stop us now!' he shouted as CDs and shelving flew across the screen. 'NO ONE!'

# **Chapter 2**

Outside the gates of St Hope's School, Rose Gupta and her father pulled up to the kerb in the family's people carrier. Dressed in a smart business suit and tie, Mr Gupta was ready for a day at the office. In the back seat, Rose – wearing her maroon school cardigan and yellow-and-maroon-striped school tie – was shifting uncomfortably. The tuba resting on her knees weighed a ton.

'Your mother and I are really looking forward to the Music Gala this afternoon,' her dad said enthusiastically. He watched as students swarmed past the car on their way into the school, talking on their mobiles and chatting and laughing with each other. He frowned when he realized so many of them were wearing items of clothing that were clearly not allowed under the school's regulations. Was this the right school for his daughter?

'It might not be very good,' Rose replied glumly. She didn't want to get his hopes up. Rehearsals hadn't been going that well. In fact, her last attempt had sounded a bit like a car being smashed in a wrecker's yard.

'Nonsense,' replied Mr Gupta firmly. 'You'll be marvellous! And we'll be right there in the front row cheering you on.'

Rose's heart sank. *Why* had she ever agreed to take part?

Inside the school, St Hope's Headmaster, Mr Flatley, was engrossed in much the same conversation with one of his favourite teachers, Ms Helen Templeman.

'Everything set for this afternoon?' he asked hopefully, as they walked down the stairs towards the schoolyard.

Looking a bit frazzled, Ms Templeman juggled a guitar case in one hand and a pile of books for marking in the other. Wearing a floral scarf tied round her head and a pale green cardigan, she had a vaguely bohemian air.

'Yes,' she replied cautiously, as she nervously eyed Julian Hamley swaggering towards them. 'The children have been practising *very* hard.'

Mr Flatley followed Ms Templeman's gaze. Further down the corridor, Fifty Pence – or Julian Hamley, to anyone not bothered with entertaining his lame self-styled gangsta-rap persona – came strutting in a baseball cap and his chunky gold chain swinging round his neck. He was belting out the lyrics to his latest failed attempt at hip-hop, while one of his cronies accompanied him on human beat-box.

'*Fifty Pence is feeling good, everyone wants to see my hood. So big up respect cos music is like food.*'

Fifty Pence had confidence in the school Music

Gala. Confident it was strictly for no-hopers, that was. In his mind, *he* was the true face of music and the only one able to keep it real.

Pausing thoughtfully as Fifty Pence swaggered past, Ms Templeman added: 'Not that practice always makes perfect . . . unfortunately.'

She sighed inwardly. It was so easy to be keen on the Music Gala when the idea was first mooted, but now that the big day had arrived Ms Templeman was a little more apprehensive. Having witnessed the rap-show that had just marched down the corridor, her form's stilted progress had rather dampened her spirits.

Outside, Rose's face was pinched with worry and her arm ached from lugging her increasingly heavy tuba around.

Rose was so busy concentrating on getting to class without breaking her back that she hardly noticed her classmates Blane Whittaker and Daisy Millar sidle up behind her. In a chivalrous gesture, Blane grabbed the handle of the tuba case and lifted it from Rose's grasp.

Rose glanced over her shoulder. 'Thanks,' she said, genuinely relieved.

'You're not playing in that stupid Gala thing, are you?' asked Blane, walking awkwardly as he carried the over-sized instrument.

'Yeah, in front of the whole school?' added Daisy.

Rose nodded mournfully.

'What are you playing?' asked Blane, genuinely

interested. When he wasn't watching the latest kung-fu movies, he loved listening to music on his MP3 player. He might even go and check out the Gala.

Rose took in Blane's funky striped T-shirt, worn casually over his white school shirt. He looked so effortlessly cool. She knew that no matter what she said, there was no way she could pretend her role in the Music Gala was going to be even remotely fashionable.

Rose could hardly get the word out.

'Beethoven,' she replied begrudgingly.

Her two classmates groaned in unison as they walked to class. The sound of a drill punctured the air and, from a distance, they could see the school caretaker, Lenny Bicknall, working hard on some brickwork. He was a familiar sight around St Hope's, with his shabby brown jacket, blue overalls and beige woolly hat.

'You know, Rose,' Daisy offered, trying to be helpful as they headed inside towards their classroom, 'you should try getting into something more *popular*. Like, try being normal for once.'

Rose would have been offended if she hadn't been so used to Daisy thinking she knew everything about *everything*.

Rose might have been the only student at St Hope's to pay any attention to school's uniform regulations, but Daisy had no such concerns. For Daisy, fashion was like a religion and she spent a considerable portion of time each morning preparing for school. Today, for example, she was wearing a T-shirt with her favourite boy-band on the front, pulled over her school shirt. Her hair was set in bunches, while large blue rose-shaped earrings dangled from her ears.

'Yeah,' teased Blane, backing Daisy up for once. 'Classical music is so boring. I bet you're just doing it to please your parents.'

'No! I'm not!' insisted Rose.

'This whole music week is *such* a dumb idea,' scoffed Daisy. 'I mean, like, St Hope's is *full* of musical talent . . .'

Daisy's voice trailed off as Fifty Pence strutted past the window, mouthing his latest lyrics.

'. . . not!' she giggled.

Just then, Rose felt something vibrating in her pocket. Looking down, she pointed to the yellow pencil sticking out of Blane's trouser pocket. The red eraser on the end of it was flashing.

Daisy and Rose reached into their pockets and produced identical pencils, both of which were also flashing red.

'It's Lenny!' said Rose in an excited whisper.

It was obvious these pencils weren't ordinary HBs. What the three classmates held in their hands were, in fact, hi-tech Pencil Communicators. And as Rose, Daisy and Blane knew all too well, the red flashing lights could only mean one thing.

They were being summoned for another mission!

# Chapter 3

Moving as fast as they could with a giant tuba in tow, the three classmates headed down the hallway. They soon found themselves standing outside an old door, covered in peeling blue paint with a plaque reading 'Caretaker's Storeroom'.

With a quick check to make sure no one was watching them, Daisy reached up to a light switch by the door.

*Beep*!

She pressed a button hidden in a panel underneath the switch. Grasping the handle to open the door, Daisy, Blane and Rose stepped quickly inside the cluttered storeroom.

Rose headed over to a mop-head in the corner of the room and pulled it towards her. As a green arrow lit up on the front of a rusty paint tin, the three of them braced themselves. *Here they go again . . .*

As the floor fell away, they all shot downwards. As it turned out, the storeroom wasn't just an ordinary caretaker's storeroom, but it was actually a powerful elevator. And Daisy, Blane and Rose weren't just ordinary schoolkids. By the time they'd reached the bottom of the lift shaft, they'd been transformed into top-secret M.I.9 agents, their school uniforms replaced by funky black spy gear.

Lenny stood waiting for the three teenagers as they strode out of the lift, holding a remote control. He, too, had been transformed into a sophisticated M.I.9 operative, sporting a sharp suit, crisp shirt and trademark polka-dot tie. Large plasma screens flickered behind him, surrounded by the hi-tech equipment of M.I. High HQ.

'We haven't got much time,' said Lenny, by way of a greeting.

'What's up?' asked Daisy. She couldn't wait for her next assignment – it would beat boring lessons any day.

But none of them were prepared for Lenny's reply. 'Teenage zombies, that's what's up. They're on the rampage.'

Daisy pulled a face. 'What? Like I-go-out-at-night-and-eat-human-brains zombies?' she asked, lolling her head to the side and waving her arms in front like an extra from some trashy horror flick.

Blane and Rose giggled. Daisy was such a drama queen.

'Nothing so *grave*,' Lenny hit back, laughing uproariously at his own joke. He only stopped when he realized three blank faces were looking at him. 'But they *are* real and they've attacked in three towns so

71

far . . . going into music stores, smashing everything in their path.'

'Each night their numbers are increasing,' Lenny added, growing serious and moving aside to reveal an image of a teenage boy frozen on the central plasma screen. 'Here's one we managed to capture earlier.'

The boy had spiky, gelled-up hair and dark circles beneath his eyes. Lenny pressed the remote and the screen came to life.

The three teen spies watched curiously as the footage played back, revealing the boy to be sitting on a high hospital bed. Slices of light streamed in through the window's blinds behind him. They could see a doctor in a white coat sitting beside the bed, holding up a can of fizzy drink in front of the boy. But the teenager just gazed vacantly ahead, his eyes completely empty.

This was *weird*. What was wrong with this kid?

The doctor yanked off the ring pull of the can and took a slurp of the drink. The boy's face remained fixed and expressionless. Even though his mouth hung open, he didn't seem interested at all.

Trying another tack, the doctor produced a skateboard, holding it up to the boy's face. The doctor flipped it over and gave its wheels a tempting spin.

Still nothing.

The doctor looked at the catatonic youth and scratched his head.

'So, unless we act, every kid in the country's gonna end up like that?' asked Rose, as Lenny pressed 'pause'. The picture of the youth's sunken features froze in a grotesque close-up.

'Gross!' remarked Daisy, always mindful of appearances. 'I hate that goth look.'

'Your mission,' Lenny announced, 'is to discover what's turning them into zombies and to find an antidote.'

Rose, Daisy and Blane understood.

'Right!' clapped Lenny, swiftly moving on. 'Gadget time!'

As if out of nowhere, Lenny produced a black velvet jewellery box. He lifted the lid to reveal a set of intricately painted yellow and brown artificial fingernails.

'You'll find a miniature camera hidden inside these false fingernails,' he explained, handing them over to St Hope's number-one fashionista.

'Ooh, nice shade!' squealed Daisy, unable to hide her approval. 'You're learning, Leonard!'

Blane rolled his eyes. She might have been an M.I.9 agent, but Daisy was *such* a girl sometimes.

Daisy's admiration of her new accessory was interrupted by an alarm suddenly beeping on Rose's wristwatch.

'Oh no,' Rose yelped, momentarily forgetting her spy-work priorities. 'I'm late for my music rehearsal! See you later!'

Watching disapprovingly as Rose ran off towards the lift and disappeared inside, Lenny turned to his two remaining agents.

'So far we've only got one piece of evidence,' he said, holding up a DVD. 'This is CCTV footage of the teenage zombies in action.'

Daisy looked disgusted, but Blane was stoked. It was times like this that he loved being an expert in martial arts. He couldn't wait to show those zombies some of his black belt moves!

'Be warned, though,' Lenny added, bracing his charges. 'It's pretty scary stuff.'

# Chapter 4

Blane and Daisy slid the DVD Lenny had given them into the machine under the plasma screens and began trawling through the CCTV footage.

'Look at those hollow, staring eyes,' marvelled Blane, twisting a dial.

'It's like maths class on a Monday morning!' Daisy joked darkly.

'Those kids look like they've been hypnotized,' Blane noted, zooming in on one of the mindless zombies.

On screen, dozens of kids crashed through a music store, ripping apart album displays and tearing CDs from the shelves.

'Hey, look at this,' Blane said suddenly. 'Check out the shirt the kid's wearing!'

Daisy studied the shot and let out a squeal of delight. She'd recognize that stylish number anywhere . . .

'CRUSH!' she yelped.

'What's Crush?' Rose's voice came from behind them, as she suddenly re-appeared from the lift carrying her tuba.

'They're some seriously dumb boy-band who can't even play live,' snorted Blane.

*A bit like me*, Rose thought sullenly.

The rehearsal for the Music Gala just now had been a *disaster*. Ms Templeman had desperately attempted to shoehorn in some last-minute practice for her Year Nine ensemble.

But no matter how hard she'd tried, Rose just couldn't hit a right note. When her tuba finally let out the loudest, most offensive honk ever, Rose snapped. She'd even yelled at poor Ms Templeman!

'I can't do this!' she'd cried angrily, standing up and storming out the door with the hapless instrument in tow. 'I don't want to play in this stupid Gala!'

She had felt horribly guilty when Ms Templeman frantically called out after her. But anyway, she thought, wasn't her spy work more important?

Daisy's noisy protesting was enough to bring Rose back to reality. She hadn't even noticed Rose's downtrodden expression as she walked back in, as she was too busy making it clear she didn't share Blane's viewpoint.

'They're *totally* gorgeous and they have *great* songs,' Daisy was loudly declaring. 'Crush couldn't have anything to do with this zombie stuff. They're *way* too cute.'

Rose joined her fellow agents at the screen. 'There are three other kids wearing the same T-shirt,' she pointed out. 'I don't think we can ignore that kind of evidence.'

Rose leaned over Blane's shoulder and twisted a dial so that the image moved to one of the cameras that focused on some youths by the tills. 'Look – when you zoom in, we see what they're buying.'

On the screen, zombie hands were fighting at each other in a battle to grab at the contents of a pile full of CDs. They all had been released by Crush.

Blane's mind was made up. 'Time to check out the pretty boys,' he said. If only Daisy didn't look so – well – *crushed*!

In his Boogie Corp office, Tony Frisco was happily watching the zombies' progress on the giant plasma screens. He'd been so engrossed in viewing the havoc raining down across Britain that he hadn't even noticed little trails of perspiration racing across his shiny scalp and forming a damp patch on the shoulders of his loud striped shirt.

Finally, Frisco chuckled, this was what it was like to know real success!

# Chapter 5

Blane flicked through the blue and pink magazine, turning up his top lip. How could Daisy actually read this rubbish? Blane baulked at the sight of the three members of Crush gazing at him soulfully on the cover. At least he could relate to one of the topics inside – if any of his mates caught him reading a girls' magazine, it would have landed him straight into 'Your Confessions! Crate-loads of Cringes!'

'I don't believe it!' Daisy sniggered joyfully as she perched on the chair beside him. 'Blane Whittaker is reading *Girly Talk*!'

'Purely for research,' Blane said trying to sound casual. 'Look! There's an article on Crush in this edition and it lists all their tour dates.'

Blane held out the page sporting a photo of the band members, all of whom were wearing sunglasses. A long list of dates filled the page.

'Check this out,' he said. 'Folkestone, Lowestoft, Bury St Edmunds. Ring any bells?'

'They're the same towns where the zombie attacks occurred!' Rose exclaimed.

'Their next gig's the biggest one on the tour,' Blane read, scanning through the dates. 'Wembley on the 24th.'

The three teen spies looked at each other in shock.

'But that's today!' Daisy cried.

'And Wembley Stadium holds a hundred thousand!' added Rose. 'If we don't get this sorted fast, there's going to be a whole lot more zombies roaming the streets by tonight!'

Just as M.I. High were making their discovery at head-quarters, tensions were brewing in the Crush tour bus as it sped along the motorway towards London.

'Darran,' huffed Gary, shooting his band-mate an accusatory stare, 'have you been using my *Hint of Blonde* again?'

The three teen-idols were sitting round a table strewn with empty cans and paper at the back of the bus, orange curtains pulled across the windows. Gary, Darran and Arran were all wearing striped, short-sleeved tops, which made them look a bit like Tweedledum and Tweedledee. And their cousin, Tweedledumber.

'I never touched your *Hint of Blonde*,' protested Darran, instinctively reaching up to check that his bottle-blonde quiff was still perfectly poised at a ninety-degree angle. 'Tell him, Arran.'

Arran looked at Darran blankly. Gary exploded.

'Well, stick to your own haircare products in future, yeah!' Gary screamed, charging at Darran. Darran dodged him, but made a grab for the *Hint of Blonde* bottle. Why should Gary get all the highlights?

'STOP THIS NONSENSE AT ONCE!'

The boys broke apart as Tony Frisco strode furiously down the bus towards them. The roar of his voice silenced the squabble in an instant. Frisco glowered at them.

'Darran,' he commanded, addressing the Crush star like a five-year-old. 'Give Gary back his hair gel'.

Darran begrudgingly returned the bottle to Gary.

'And, Gary, stop pushing Darran,' ordered Frisco, before turning his attention to Arran. Arran had remained sitting at the table throughout the drama without saying a single word.

'Arran! You've got chocolate on your shirt!' snapped Frisco, as he noticed the brown smears trailing from Arran's chin and down his front.

Gary and Darran suppressed giggles as a shame-faced Arran wiped away the chocolate.

'Didn't I tell you boys to learn those song lyrics?' added Frisco, hissing. 'You've got a very important gig tonight and I need you to be word perfect. Understand?'

The boys looked at each other anxiously. It didn't pay to make Tony Frisco angry.

'Yes, Mr Frisco,' they replied in a collective whisper, watching the back of their record-label boss as he charged towards the front of the bus.

\* \* \*

Deep in the underground M.I. High headquarters, Daisy and Rose observed Blane as he held the palms of his hands out in front of him, slowly rotating his body round. He was practising his t'ai chi moves.

'He says it helps him think,' Rose grinned at Daisy, rolling her eyes.

Blane pushed his palms forward smoothly.

'We need to get Crush into St Hope's to check 'em out,' he said thoughtfully.

'They'd never visit a dump like this in a zillion years,' groaned Daisy.

'Maybe not,' agreed Rose. 'But if they're playing Wembley Stadium tonight . . . a couple of well-placed diversions could send them our way.'

Daisy's face lit up as the realization hit her. If they could pull this off, she'd get to meet . . .

'CRUSH!' she squealed, spinning round in her chair. 'I'm going to meet Crush!'

Daisy kissed the picture of her heart-throbs in *Girly Talk*. She might have liked to be known for playing it cool, but this was one time Daisy didn't mind letting her exterior slip. This was going to be the greatest day of her life!

'Yeah,' said Blane, stretching his palms out and turning them in a fluid mid-air circle. 'The same Crush who are turning kids into zombies.'

'We don't know that for sure,' Daisy hit back.

'One of us needs to get close to them,' Rose suggested. 'Study their body language, find out what effect they're having on people and how they're doing it.'

'That'll be *moi*,' beamed Daisy happily, practically falling out of her chair.

'No way,' protested Blane, halting his meditation and dropping his hands. 'You're a fan. We need someone who's totally objective.'

Daisy raised her eyes skywards. Just like Blane to stop her fun . . . had *Girly Talk* gone to his head?

'Wrong!' she said firmly. She was going to get to meet her idols, no matter what. 'Going undercover needs *specialist* knowledge, and that's what I've got – and *you* haven't.'

'Yeah? Prove it!' Blane challenged.

Lenny emerged from the shadows. He had been listening to the bickering and knew there was only one way to put a stop to it. Assuming the role of quizmaster, he motioned to Daisy and Blane to take seats next to each other in the middle of the room.

Daisy and Blane hurriedly settled into their chairs, clutching their Pencil Communicators. With the flashing red eraser ends, the pencils made perfect makeshift buzzers. Daisy narrowed her eyes as she looked at Blane. *She wasn't going to let him win this!*

'Gary hates . . .' Lenny began, kicking off the first round, 'all vegetables *except* . . .?'

*BZZZZ!*

Lenny looked expectantly at Blane.

'Himself?' the male teen agent answered, allowing a sly smile. Daisy rolled her eyes.

Lenny moved on to question two. 'Arran hasn't spoken in public since . . .?'

Daisy quickly hit her buzzer.

'May the 12th, 2001,' she trilled. 'He plugged his hairdryer into a wet socket.'

'*Correct.*' Lenny pressed on. 'Darran is allergic to . . .?'

Blane was the first to buzz.

'Talent?' he offered, sarcastically.

Lenny ignored him and read out question four. 'How many downloads of the new single have there been?'

Daisy confidently waved her Pencil Communicator.

'Forty million, six hundred and thirty-six,' she beamed triumphantly.

'OK, OK!' conceded Blane, holding his hands in the air. 'I give up!'

Daisy felt dizzy with elation. She'd won! Forget saving Britain from a zombie attack. She was going undercover to *meet Crush*!

'Now can we deal with the Crush tour bus?' Rose pleaded.

Rose wasn't interested in meeting some vain boy-band. She just had to get Blane and Daisy to refocus on the mission. If they didn't take action soon, it wouldn't be long before Britain was completely overrun with zombies.

# Chapter 6

Blane inched along the cement wall by the motorway, training his binoculars on the busy road ahead of him. With Daisy protesting profusely, both Blane and Rose had figured if at least one of the members of Crush lacked the sense to know that water and electricity didn't mix, then the rest of them couldn't be too smart either. M.I. High had a plan that just might work.

Blane could see the Crush coach heading towards him. It wasn't easy to miss. A massive orange-and-white Crush logo swirled against a bright green background on the side of the bus.

Blane quickly crouched down and held up a massive sign: 'THIS WAY TO WEMBLEY'.

Inside the Crush coach, the confused bus driver slammed on the brakes and hit his indicator, turning off at the next exit. He hadn't expected to see the road sign so soon.

Further down the road, he spotted a sign saying 'NOT FAR NOW' in large letters.

'NEARLY THERE!' encouraged the next one.

The bewildered driver obeyed the road signs without

a second thought, as he was unfamiliar with the area. It wasn't long before he found himself driving down a quiet residential road, hopelessly lost.

The driver put on the brakes and leaned out of the window, looking for a passer-by to ask for directions. Three teenagers wearing Crush T-shirts and hoodies came rambling along the pavement.

'Excuse me!' he called, as they came level with the bus. 'I'm looking for Wembley Stadium.'

The three kids didn't even bother to look up. They just kept walking, staring straight ahead.

'Kids today,' muttered the driver, firing up the bus and deciding to try further down the road. 'They're all zombies – the lot of them!'

A very short distance away on the front steps of St Hope's School, Mr Flatley stood looking out into the street uncertainly, surrounded by a gaggle of pupils. Daisy hopped from one foot to the other beside him.

Excited yelps broke out among the children as the Crush tour bus rounded a corner and came into view.

'Here's the group I was telling you about, Sir,' gushed Daisy. 'CRUSH! If you get them to play in the Gala concert, it will be like the most amazing thing ever!'

'Right,' nodded Mr Flatley. 'And they're really famous, you say?'

'*Really* famous?' spluttered Daisy. *Mr Flatley was so stuck in 1995!* 'They're superstars!'

The bus juddered against the kerb, the doors

swinging open as it ground to a halt. Tony Frisco stepped on to the pavement and studied the surroundings. He was clearly bothered.

The kids on the steps of St Hope's started screaming hysterically.

'Wait!' Frisco tried to shout above the din. He was taking off his glasses now, realization dawning on his face.

'This isn't Wembley!' he bellowed.

But the Crush boys were already emerging from the bus and St Hope's pupils were about to lose any last vestiges of decorum they'd had.

The entire school went crazy. Students streamed forward towards their pop heroes, girls yelling and shrieking frantically. Mr Flatley, with his greying hair and sensible checked jacket, was sent flying awkwardly into the bedlam.

'Careful, careful!' shouted Frisco desperately. He had to keep his pop property in one piece for their Wembley gig. 'Those boys are worth a lot of money!'

Luckily for Blane, Frisco was too busy watching his precious cargo as they worked the crowd to notice him sneaking round the rear of the tour bus. Crush were in full pop-star mode now, shaking every hand that grabbed at them and signing autographs.

Reaching under the wheel arch at the back of the bus, Blane felt around and gave something an almighty tug. It ripped free. Blane held it up with satisfaction – it was the bus's alternator. The Crush boys wouldn't be going anywhere for a while.

Back in the pandemonium, Mr Flatley got back up on his feet and approached Tony Frisco.

'Hello,' he said, greeting the mogul cheerfully. 'I'm Mr Flatley – the Headmaster.'

'Tony Frisco, Crush Master,' Frisco replied, scowling. 'I . . . I mean manager.'

Mr Flatley was too preoccupied to pay attention to Tony Frisco's strange reply. Judging by the chaos around him, Daisy had been right. Just last week the Prime Minister had arrived on his doorstep to present the Bravekidz Awards, and now here were Britain's favourite pop-band to play the Music Gala! What a coup for St Hope's!

Mr Flatley indicated the entrance to the school. 'If you'll come this way . . .' he said, brimming with pride.

Blane had returned from his mission and was watching the back of the Boogie Corp man as he slithered into school. Blane stood next to Daisy's best mates, Kaleigh and Zara, as the two girls gazed dreamily at their pop heroes.

'Tony Frisco, who's he?' Blane wondered out loud.

'Crush's *manager*,' replied Kaleigh scornfully. Sometimes Blane could be just as dorky as his geekoid friend Stewart. 'He was some one-hit wonder – my mum used to love him.'

Blane pulled a face. '*He* used to be a singer?'

'Who cares?' replied Zara, turning on her heals and heading into the throng after Darran. 'The man *I'm* going to marry is going *that* way.'

The Crush boys were now striding through the school, waving at their legion of St Hope's fans. The route was lined with girls, begging for autographs and screaming excitedly. It was even too much for Mrs Nolan, the large ladle-waving dinner lady, who fainted as they passed right by her.

'It was so kind of you to agree to perform at our Gala,' Mr Flatley was saying gratefully, walking a short distance behind the commotion with Tony Frisco.

'Gala?' spat Frisco. 'What Gala? We've got a gig to perform at Wembley tonight!'

'Oh, don't worry,' Mr Flatley soothed, not noticing the mogul's confusion. 'You'll be finished in plenty of time. You're onstage at half past one. Now, we've set aside the art room for you and the boys.'

Tony Frisco followed the Headmaster down the corridor, but his mind was elsewhere. He still couldn't understand it. How had they ended up here and not at Wembley?

Down in M.I. High HQ, Blane desperately searched for clues.

'What are you doing?' asked Rose. She hadn't been the least bit interested in watching the girls make idiots of themselves falling over Crush.

'Research,' Blane replied, flicking a switch on the

keyboard. 'Whoever's behind this, it isn't Crush. Those boys are as dense as an Amazonian rainforest.'

'Have you got any better suggestions?' Rose pressed.

'It's just a hunch,' mused Blane. 'But I was wondering about Tony Frisco – the ex-pop star?'

'What about checking out the records of those old talent shows?' Rose suggested. 'Plenty of one-hit wonders there.'

'Excellent work, Rose, but I'm afraid you're going to have to hold off the investigating for now.' Rose's heart sank as Lenny appeared through the door, carrying her tuba case. She didn't have to ask him what this was going to be about.

'The concert's about to begin and you're due onstage,' Lenny added cheerily. 'We don't want any awkward questions now, do we?'

Rose sighed wearily and reluctantly took the case. There wasn't any way out of this – she'd have to go and face the music. Or lack, thereof . . .

# Chapter 7

The Crush boys strolled into the art room, quickly followed by their eagle-eyed manager.

'Get back to learning those lines, boys!' commanded Tony Frisco, clapping his hands.

The Crush lads exchanged withering looks. Mr Frisco was always bossing them around, wanting them to learn his stupid song lyrics.

'Why can't we sing our own words like we used to?' asked Gary hesitantly.

Frisco's mouth twisted into an angry scowl. Darran thought he saw a flicker of hurt flash across his boss's face.

'You boys question *me*?' Frisco demanded.

Realizing their mistake, the boys looked contrite.

'Who was it who first discovered you busking in that smelly subway?' cried Frisco, edging towards them.

'You, Mr Frisco,' replied Darran, looking down at his shoes.

'Who was it that took you and moulded you into stars?' he said, raising his voice louder. The hurt had quickly been replaced by fury.

'You, Mr Frisco,' conceded Gary.

'Changed your clothes and styled your hair?'

The boys knew they didn't have a leg to stand on. Gary silently reached up and nervously twirled his highlights.

'You, Mr Frisco,' mouthed Arran, his shoulders drooping with resignation.

Frisco walked over to gaze out of one of the art room's windows.

'Was it a crime for me to want to protect you from the cruel world out there?' snarled Frisco, his face contorted in pain. 'You've no idea what it's like! How fickle the critics can be; how the critics can eat you up and spit you out like . . . like . . .'

He was momentarily stuck for words.

'Like those nuts with shells that Arran likes?' offered Gary.

'Pistachios!' remembered Frisco, spinning round. 'Yes, something like that.'

The boys shrunk back as their manager began marching towards them.

'Well, it *won't* happen again,' he spat, staring them down. 'Now get back to work!'

Frisco held two fingers behind his ear and leaned forward threateningly.

'UMM?' he thundered. 'I CAN'T HEAR YOU!'

'Yes, Mr Frisco,' replied the Crush boys in unison, any idea of a mutiny quashed. It *really* didn't pay to make Mr Frisco angry.

\* \* \*

On the other side of the art-room door, Fifty Pence was doing a brisk trade in black-market Crush merchandise. He knew a business opportunity when he saw one. The second he'd heard the simpering boy-band were coming to St Hope's, he'd got one of his mates to set him up with loads of T-shirts, posters, CDs and anything else he could get his hands on. There was a frantic crowd of girls and female teachers besieging his makeshift stall.

'Ladies, please, calm down! There's enough for everyone!' yelled Fifty Pence, working the floor like an East End watch dealer. 'That's right! Get your official Crush merchandise!'

Rose's parents stood a few metres away, watching Fifty Pence's mini-market with a mixture of wariness and mirth. They'd arrived at St Hope's minutes ago in anticipation of the Music Gala.

'Rose said she'd meet us here,' Mr Gupta said to his wife, wondering once again why his talented eldest daughter insisted on going to a school that included sloppily dressed students who were openly dealing contraband in the corridor. 'This is such a proud day to have a real virtuoso in the family.'

Mr Gupta was genuinely looking forward to seeing his daughter play. As he scanned his surroundings, Mr Gupta was just delighted at the large number of pupils who looked as excited as he felt. It was obvious they were *all* coming to see Rose play in the Gala.

At that moment, Rose stepped out into the corridor

carrying her tuba. She froze when she saw her parents, standing beside Fifty Pence's makeshift stall.

'And look at all these children come to listen to her play her tuba,' Rose heard her dad say happily to her mother, as he cautiously picked up a miniature Darran doll.

Rose was suddenly terrified. Her poor parents . . . they didn't realize that the crowds were there for one thing and one thing only – Crush!

Rose felt sick as her eyes followed the hordes of students heading for the hall. Performing on her foghorn tuba was bad enough, but now she'd have to do it in front of the *whole* school – lured to the Gala by the chance to see Crush. She just couldn't do this.

Rose turned on her heels and hurried down the hallway, in the opposite direction from her parents.

Back inside the art room, Tony Frisco was still laying down the law. He had just one final instruction for the band before heading outside to sort some business – lock the door and don't let *anyone* in.

Frisco left the room, pausing to listen as the lock turned dutifully in the keyhole on the other side of the door. Smugly satisfied, the manager pulled out his mobile phone and marched off down the corridor.

Daisy watched as Frisco left the art room. She'd been pressed against the wall underneath an archway, hidden out of view. But now Daisy was starting to get excited. She was going to meet Crush any second!

'Daisy,' Rose's voice crackled through Daisy's Pencil Communicator as she issued instructions from M.I. High HQ. 'Watch out for Crush trying out any hypnotism on you. And don't look into their eyes,' she added.

'Hey!' Daisy replied indignantly, preparing to put the pencil back in her pocket. Honestly, Rose could be such a worry-meister. 'I *am* a professional.'

Rose was keeping tabs on Daisy on one of the large M.I. High plasma screens. A picture of her co-agent outside the art room beamed back at her. Rose sighed as she watched Daisy preening herself, ready to meet her idols.

Daisy threw her shoulders back and knocked on the art-room door.

'Hello?' she heard nervous voices call.

'Hi, guys,' called Daisy cheerily. 'Can you let me in a moment?'

'We're . . . not allowed to let anyone in,' Gary replied, trying to sound firm. On the other side of the door, the three teen heart-throbs looked at each other uncertainly. Mr Frisco had said no. But this girl sounded kinda cute.

'It's only for an autograph,' sang Daisy, pleading. 'It's for my little sister. She really *loves* you guys.'

There was a brief silence before Daisy heard the key turning in the lock. *Too easy!* The door opened. There, right in front of her, were the three members of the cutest band on the planet.

*Oh my . . . !* Daisy's thoughts trailed off as she reacted the only way she could.

She fainted.

# Chapter 8

'Daisy!' shouted Rose, staring helplessly as Gary caught Daisy just before she hit the floor. But she was out for the count. Rose watched the plasma screen helplessly as Gary dragged Daisy inside the art room.

'SCHOOL MUSIC WEEK – LET'S HIT THE RIGHT NOTES TOGETHER!'

A large banner swung above the students crowded into St Hope's school hall. The place was almost full as Rose's parents took their seats, brimming with pride. Onstage, two pupils were just coming to the end of their recorder duet, a rather grim rendition of 'Three Blind Mice'. It was depressing to watch.

Backstage, Ms Templeman was beside herself with worry.

'You haven't seen Rose anywhere?' she asked Tina and Tanya, the only other two members of her Year Nine ensemble. 'I do hope her nerves haven't got the better of her. It's just not like Rose to let anyone down.'

But Rose was nowhere to be seen. Ms Templeman

looked on anxiously as Mr Flatley mounted the stairs to the stage and banged his head against the microphone. The mike was far too high for him, but instead of lowering the stand he spoke up into it, stretching his neck out like an ostrich. The microphone protested with a loud squeal of feedback.

'Er . . . well done, Colin and Lyndsay, for . . . er . . . an interesting recorder interpretation of, um . . . whatever it was,' Mr Flatley stammered, flustered by all the excitement. 'Anyway – coming up soon, we have our special guests, The Crush!'

None of the students noticed the Headmaster get the name of the band wrong. They were too busy going wild with screams and shrieks of delight.

'All right, all right,' instructed Mr Flatley, trying to restore calm. 'Settle down, boys and girls.'

'To keep us entertained until then,' he added, looking expectantly to the wings of the stage. 'A little Beethoven. Yes, please welcome on stage . . . er . . . Tina and Tanya Jones and Rose Gupta!'

As Daisy came to, she thought she must be dreaming. Lying on the floor of the art room, she opened her eyes to be greeted with the sight of the three Crush boys' faces peering down at her.

'Er, are you all right?' asked Gary, genuinely concerned.

'I think so,' replied Daisy sheepishly, fluttering her eyelids. 'I must have fainted, but I'm OK now.'

As the boys helped her up, Daisy quickly pulled her Pencil Communicator out of her pocket.

'It's not like I've been *hypnotized* or anything,' she said loudly, for the benefit of Blane and Rose listening in at M.I. High HQ.

'Any chance of an autograph?' Daisy added, passing the pencil to Arran. 'You can make it to Daisy – your number-one fan, the one with the cute smile.'

Returning from some urgent caretaker work stemming from the Crush-induced chaos, Lenny was surprised to find Rose in front of the plasma screen, listening out for signals from Daisy at M.I. High HQ.

'You're back already?' he asked, walking out from the lift. 'How did the Beethoven go?'

'Um . . . fine,' lied Rose, very mindful that she'd missed her spot. Her parents would most probably be freaking out by now.

'How's Daisy getting on?' Lenny said, hoping she'd remembered the mission and wasn't caught up in the hysteria in the hall.

'OK,' replied Rose. 'There's no sign of anyone using hypnosis on her. She did lose it for a moment, but that was just because she was so close to Crush.'

'What about their recorded music?' asked Lenny, studying the green peaks and troughs of the sound waves that Rose was currently watching on screen.

'I'm looking at its waved forms and there's nothing suspicious,' reported Rose. 'I'm hoping Daisy can find out something more. But if it's not the music and it's not hypnosis, then what is it?'

Blane called over from the other side of the headquarters. From the footage he'd just discovered, he was pretty sure he knew the answer to that question.

'Tony Frisco,' he said confidently. 'That's what! Check this out.'

Twisting a dial on a computer, Blane began to play a clip from an old TV show.

An image of a much younger Tony Frisco holding a microphone filled the screen, as he stood belting out a song in front of a yellow sign bearing the words 'POP FACTOR'. He was wearing an ugly crushed-velvet suit and his hair was a mass of wild orange curls.

Frisco tunelessly croaked the last words of his song into the microphone and then fell melodramatically to his knees.

The sound of silence was deafening. But that was nothing compared to the thunder of booing and jeering that followed.

The next image showed Frisco standing in front of a judging panel. He might as well be in a firing line, thought Blane.

'It was cheesy, it was plastic, you're past your sell-by-date,' chided an unseen judge to uproarious laughter from the audience. 'I'm sorry, but you've got no future in this business.'

Frisco looked mortally wounded, as though he

was about to burst out crying. But, all of a sudden, he seemed to lose his cool.

'Tony Frisco will be back one day!' he shouted defiantly, making his way off the stage. 'I will have the biggest selling single of all time! You'll see!'

Just as he neared the edge, Frisco couldn't stop himself from turning round to add: 'You SMELL! I'll be back. You'll see!'

Rose winced as the footage finished. That could so easily have been her, up onstage at the Music Gala today!

'Poor man,' she murmured. 'How terrible to be humiliated like that in public.'

'He got just what he deserved,' Blane decided. 'It's people like him that kill *real* music.'

'Yeah, he must have ended up very bitter and twisted,' Rose said.

Blane grabbed his things and headed for the lift.

'It's time he and I had a little chat.'

# Chapter 9

As Blane entered the lift, Rose turned her attention back to Daisy's Crush mission in the art room. Through the Pencil Communicator, Rose could hear Gary attempting to fulfil Daisy's autograph request.

The hapless pop star was having problems spelling Daisy's name. His tongue hung out as he wrote slowly.

'"Daisy", yes . . . and there's a letter "i" in there too!' Daisy offered helpfully.

As Gary finally completed his autograph, Daisy spied a sheet of paper in Darran's hand.

'What's that?' she asked.

'The words to our new single,' Gary explained. 'Mr Frisco always makes us sing it live, but the words are really hard to remember.'

'We have to sing some bits of the song louder than others,' chipped in Darran, placing the lyrics down on the art table.

'But he's *obsessed* with us singing this one particular song,' mused Gary.

Daisy was intrigued. 'Really?' she asked.

Rose could smell a rat.

'Daisy,' she instructed, speaking into the Pencil Communicator. 'Get the fingernail cam on those lyrics!'

Daisy quickly ran the back of her hand over the sheet of paper.

'Hey! What are you doing?' demanded Darran, looking at her suspiciously.

'I just got them painted,' beamed Daisy, holding up her fingernails for the boys to admire, desperately trying to cover her tracks. 'Cool colour, huh?'

Gary and Darran looked at Daisy with their mouths wide open. They weren't buying her little fashion show. Arran twirled his finger round his ear, implying Daisy was a bit of a fruitcake.

Meanwhile, the pictures from the cam began to appear on Rose's screen. She read them out to Lenny.

> *Look into my eyes,*
> *Believe in only me,*
> *Oh baby, oh baby.*
> *I feel a kind of rush,*
> *Whenever I'm by Crush.*

Rose's fingers flew over the keyboard as she inputted the lyrics into a computer.

'*Only you can understand . . .*' she continued, typing. '*Why this love cannot be banned. You are my number one. All others are now gone.*'

'There's an old technique for influencing people, called subliminal messaging,' Rose told Lenny – finally realizing she was on to something. 'They used it in adverts till it got banned. Certain key words are given undue emphasis in the rhyming pattern. Like the "obey" part of "oh baby".'

Rose hit a key and the letters 'oh ba' were instantly highlighted in red.

'And "*B-U-Y* Crush", as in *purchase* the single – not stand next to them,' she mused, going back through the lyrics. Suddenly, Rose's eyes widened. *That was it – this wasn't a single, it was an order!*

'So, Crush have been creating zombies via their lyrics?' asked Lenny, putting Rose's thoughts into words.

'I'm sure of it,' confirmed Rose. 'Now I just need to find some way of overcoming the hidden messages!'

# Chapter 10

Daisy heard Rose's voice in her ear.

'Daisy,' Rose instructed firmly. 'You have to keep Crush in the art room. They mustn't be allowed to perform live.'

Daisy rushed over to the art-room door, turned the key and pulled it out of the lock.

The Crush boys stared at her with bewildered expressions.

'Are you some sort of stalker?' asked Gary, finally.

'No!' Daisy protested, aware how weird her behaviour must now be looking. 'I just wanna hang out with you guys.'

Gary wasn't convinced. This girl might be pretty cute, but she was seriously starting to freak him out.

'That's it!' Gary decided. 'I'm ringing Mr Frisco!'

Agent Millar turned away in a panic and spoke frantically into her Pencil Communicator.

'Rose!' she hissed. 'You *have* to hurry. I can't keep them here much longer!'

The boys' mouths fell open.

'Now she's talking to herself,' whispered Darran to Arran and Gary, growing alarmed.

'She's bonkers!' cried Gary.

It was all too much for Darran. 'Look, you have to let us out of here!' he insisted desperately. 'Give us back the key.'

Daisy fluttered her eyelids and flashed them a dazzling smile. Hurrying to an open art-room window, she threw her arm out carelessly and let the key drop.

'Oops!' she said, holding her hand to her mouth in fake distress.

Elsewhere in the school, Tony Frisco was trying to hold a conversation on his mobile phone as noise from the Music Gala emanated around St Hope's.

'Sorry, it's still too noisy in here,' he spoke into the handset, spying the quiet of an empty music room and letting himself inside. He held the phone closer to his ear and strode over to look out one of the windows.

'So, the single's still number one?' he asked with a maniacal grin.

Outside, Blane crept up to the door of the room, eavesdropping on Frisco's conversation. He could hear Rose as she came through on his Pencil Communicator, speaking urgently.

'Blane, you were right,' she said breathlessly. 'It's Tony Frisco's lyrics turning kids into zombies.'

'Check,' her co-agent replied, entering and scooting across the room as Frisco's back was turned and hiding behind the piano. 'I'm on to him now.'

Blane could hear Frisco's voice rising in excitement as he continued his phone call.

'We're getting even closer to having the biggest single of all time,' he warbled. 'And we'll have even more zombies to help us after the Wembley gig. Great. Bye.'

Frisco turned to see the piano sitting in the corner of the room. This was the perfect time to unleash his super-silky vocal skills and celebrate his outstanding achievements. Frisco practically skipped across to the instrument and began thumping tunelessly at the keys.

*The Boogieman is number one,*
*His rising sales go on and on . . .*

Frisco's voice became a screeching wail. The pain was too much for Blane.

'Not any more!' he interrupted, leaping out from behind the piano.

'Says who?' sneered Frisco. Who was this kid? And why hadn't he been turned into a zombie?

'Says another of your many critics,' Blane informed him. 'No one *chooses* to buy that rubbish you and Crush churn out.'

'That's big talk, indie kid,' snapped Frisco, darting

over to the doors of the music room and pulling them shut. He pointed a menacing finger at Blane.

'You're going nowhere!'

Daisy, meanwhile, was having problems of her own. She could tell she was running out of time in the art room.

'Rose, how's it going?' she hissed as she turned her back to talk into her Pencil Communicator. 'Can I let them go yet?'

The Crush boys looked at Daisy in horror.

'She's talking to herself again,' Darran said with a deeply disturbed expression.

'Look,' said Gary, using his best negotiating-with-a-lunatic voice. 'Let us out and we won't press charges.'

'Yeah,' Darran agreed. 'We'll try to get you help. Mr Frisco knows all the top showbiz shrinks.'

But it wasn't just the Crush boys who were worried. Daisy was running out of ideas. Without any backup, she'd have to take matters into her own hands. She lunged forward and snatched the lyric sheet from Arran's hand, stuffing it into her mouth.

Daisy attempted her best winning smile as she vigorously chewed on the paper and then began to swallow it. Darran, Arran and Gary stared at each other, completely aghast. Talk about taking the cake and eating it too!

All of a sudden, they heard a key turning in the

lock on the other side of the door. The boys let out a desperate cry of 'HELLLP!' as Mr Flatley came bustling inside.

'Ah, loosening up the old vocal chords, I hear?' beamed the Headmaster, misinterpreting the band's plea as a pre-concert rehearsal. Mr Flatley joined in, singing his own completely-out-of-tune scale.

'I do hope you weren't trying to keep them all to yourself, Daisy?' Mr Flatley added, scolding Daisy good-humouredly.

Instead of speaking, Daisy belched, just as the three teen-idols dived behind Mr Flatley and made for the door. They'd do anything to get away from this crazy stalker girl.

Once at a safe distance, Gary turned round triumphantly.

'Bad luck, psycho!' he jeered from the doorway, defiantly holding up a piece of paper.

Daisy's heart sank as she recognized it as another copy of the zombie lyrics. But it was too late to do anything. Crush were already halfway down the corridor, flanked by a trail of giggling schoolgirls.

Mr Flatley was too thrilled by the next event to notice anything untoward had just happened right in front of him. He smiled broadly at Daisy as he turned from the room.

'SHOWTIME!' he declared, marching off towards the hall like an exuberant ringmaster.

# Chapter 11

'Tony *Boogieman* Frisco,' Blane jeered. 'The failed Pop Factor contestant.'

Frisco eyed the M.I. High agent suspiciously as the two inched towards each other in St Hope's music room. Frisco was desperate for some form of weapon to help him get rid of this little pest. He grabbed for the first thing he could lay his hands on – a pair of red maracas.

'Oh, I didn't *fail*,' he spat. 'Those idiot judges were tone-deaf!'

Frisco lunged towards Blane, thrusting the maracas from side to side in the spy's face.

Blane grabbed two large snare drumsticks and twirled them around in a swift martial-arts movement.

'Lowest score in the history of the show, wasn't it?' he mocked, knowing how much the fact would infuriate Frisco. 'But then that's what your rubbish music deserves.'

Frisco thrust at him again with the maracas, but Blane swiped them away with his sticks.

'And now you've stooped to brainwashing kids to try and sell your cheesy pop?' Blane continued.

Frisco threw aside the maracas, grabbing a trombone instead. Blane ducked as a trombone arm narrowly missed his head.

'Think of it as re-educating the public,' Frisco snarled, taking another swipe at Blane.

'You're a useless old has-been!' Blane swapped his sticks for a pair of giant cymbals and crashed them together in a deafening thud.

'Who's about to have the biggest-selling single of all time?' Frisco shouted hysterically. 'And then we're going to be working on operas and easy-listening ballads too, and pretty soon the whole world is going to be listening to my music and nothing else!'

'That's not what music's about!' Blane shouted. 'It's about self-expression. Freedom of choice!'

'I don't think so!' Frisco yelled, laughing like a madman and yet again powering the trombone arm towards Blane. 'As my boys are about to prove!'

The insane situation in the music room was nothing compared to the bedlam that was breaking out in the school hall as the three heart-throbs from Crush appeared in the doorway. To a deafening wall of crying and screams, Gary, Darran and Arran hurried down the central aisle. Now their terrifying ordeal with the crazed stalker in the art room was over, they were glad to be back on more familiar territory.

Mr Flatley stood to the side of the stage, well prepared. He'd stuffed generous chunks of cotton wool into his ears as a protective measure against the imminent racket.

As the band made it to the stage, a door at the back of the hall swung open as Daisy raced in. She'd come well armed too, wearing a pair of stylish grey earmuffs to block out the zombie-inducing music.

Daisy sped down the side of the hall and made straight for the sound desk onstage. Frantically, she reached for the leads connecting the speaker system. If Daisy shut down the sound, then no one could get brainwashed.

But the lead wouldn't budge. Daisy tried to tug it harder, but to her surprise someone suddenly grabbed her arm, pulling it out of the way. Daisy swung round and couldn't believe who she saw.

It was one of her best friends, Kaleigh, looking furious!

'Hey!' snapped Kaleigh. 'Just cos Gary fancies *me*!'

Daisy glanced back at the wire, desperately trying to figure out what to do. Her other best friend, Zara, appeared next to the sound desk.

'You mean me!' Zara argued, looking at Kaleigh.

Mr Flatley moved swiftly forward to break up the argument.

'Girls!' he exclaimed. 'I don't like this *popular* music either, but please return to your seats . . .'

Just as Mr Flatley finished his sentence, music began to pour out of the speakers. Crush were about to start . . .

Daisy watched with a heavy heart as Kaleigh, Zara

and Mr Flatley hurried into the audience. She'd have to think of something else. Daisy raced off towards the back of the hall as Gary started singing.

'*Look into my eyes*,' he warbled. '*Look into my eyes, believe in only me.*'

'*Oh baby, oh baby, oh baby.*'

In the audience, a boy's head twitched.

'*I feel a kind of rush*,' crooned Gary.

Mr Gupta's eyes started to glaze over as his head lolled to one side.

'*Whenever I'm by Crush.*'

All across the audience, pupils were suddenly rising to their feet. Their arms stretched out in front of them and all had the same blank look to their eyes.

'*Only you can understand . . .*'

Mr Flatley was in the front row, swaying from side to side. He was enjoying this more than he'd expected. *Maybe if he took out his cotton-wool earplugs he could hear it even better . . .* Mr Flatley let out a small groan as his eyes glazed over.

'*So look into my eyes, look into my eyes . . .*'

Ms Templeman finally dropped the pile of books she'd been carrying around all day. Her arms stretched out in front of her.

Daisy couldn't watch any more. But she knew she had to keep everyone in the same place. She ran outside and pulled the hall doors shut. Almost too late, she reeled round in horror to see a zombified Fifty Pence heading straight for her.

'Blane? Rose?' she called, urgently pulling out her Pencil Communicator. 'Where *are* you?'

At least one of Daisy's fellow agents was down in M.I. High HQ, frantically trying to answer a question of her own.

'Negation factor three over ten,' mumbled Rose to herself, furiously scribbling mathematical formulae on a whiteboard. 'Positive imagery – two point eight; this antidote song better work.'

Agent Whittaker was still up in the music room, fighting off an increasingly fierce Tony Frisco. But as he held up a cymbal to protect himself from another swipe of the trombone, Blane suddenly spotted just the right weapon. Abandoning the cymbals, he grabbed a maroon electric guitar plugged into a practice amp by a desk. He instantly started to rip into a raucously loud riff.

Tony Frisco's face crumpled in distress as he dropped the trombone and covered his ears.

'Stop!' he pleaded.

Blane bashed out some more screeching chords.

'Where's the melody?' yelled Frisco in agony. 'Where's the catchy chorus?'

Taking advantage of Frisco's disorientated state, Blane looked around for a bass drum and found one. Leaping towards Frisco, he deftly brought it crashing down on to the music mogul's shiny bald head. Frisco couldn't move. His arms were pinned to the side of his body.

Losing no time at all, Blane shoved the dazed Frisco towards the instrument storeroom, slammed the door, locked it and pocketed the key.

Taking out his Pencil Communicator, Blane shouted into it as he bolted towards the school hall.

'Hold on, Daisy!' he urged. 'I'm on my way!'

He just hoped he wasn't too late.

# Chapter 12

Blane rapped harshly on the glass door that separated the entrance of the hall from the main auditorium. He'd arrived just in time to see Daisy pushing away a zombified Fifty Pence. Behind her, he could see the hall was now completely full of zombies. Even Mr Flatley, the teachers and the ladle-waving dinner lady were wandering around in a mind-bending catatonic trance.

Daisy scrambled for the door and dragged Blane in, before pulling it shut again.

'Hey! Crush CDs over there!' shouted Blane, covering his ears with his fingers and trying to direct the zombies away from him and Daisy.

'We'll never be able to hold them!' Daisy groaned.

Blane looked over the sea of zombie heads. 'Where's Rose?'

There was an urgent knocking on the glass doors. The two agents spun round again. Had some of the zombies escaped?

But it was Rose standing outside. She was waving a sheet of paper in the air.

'She's a zombie!' exclaimed Blane.

'No,' cut in Daisy. 'It's just bad make-up. Let her in!'

Rose came inside and gave a gasp as she spotted her parents staggering around the hall.

'Do you have the antidote?' demanded Blane, yelling above the din.

'Yes,' nodded Rose, just managing to hear him with her fingers in her ears. 'It's a new set of lyrics!'

'For Crush to sing?' demanded Blane.

Rose shook her head.

'No. It's all about which words you stress and when – AAAAGH!'

Rose's explanation was rudely interrupted by the dinner lady, who had come up behind them. And now she had her muscular arms wrapped round Rose.

Blane shoved the zombie out of the way allowing Rose to finish.

'– and when you sing them,' she added. Realizing she was the only one who knew which words were important, Rose suddenly felt sick.

Oh no! She would have to sing in public!

'Well, let's go!' cried Daisy, just as Crush's song came to a spectacular end inside the hall. 'We have to get you on stage fast!'

Rose's heart sank. If she couldn't play a tuba at the Music Gala, how on earth was she going to sing a song for the very first time, in front of everyone? She hadn't skipped the Music Gala for nothing. But as she looked around the hall at the heaving mass of zombies, Rose realized the alternative was far, far worse.

Daisy and Blane shoved a path through the tangled mass of zombie bodies and finally deposited Rose at the side of the stage.

'Go and knock 'em dead!' Daisy said encouragingly. 'Er . . . *un*-dead!'

Rose slowly climbed up on to the stage and took the microphone from Gary.

'Er . . . hi,' she began, speaking nervously into it. 'Since this is the end of our school Gala, one of us has to . . . er . . . sing a song with you. And it's . . . er . . . me. Sixteen-eight time signature; metronome marking ninety-two; allegro . . .'

Darran, Arran and Gary stared at Rose in confusion. They didn't know many musical terms.

'Huh?' they shrugged.

'Oh!' Rose commanded, growing exasperated. 'Just gimme some heavy beats!'

'What? Play *live*?' asked Gary.

*It was now or never.* Rose nodded and gulped.

As a heady bass line pumped out of the speakers, Rose bobbed her head in time to the beat nervously.

'*Look away from their eyes*,' she began to sing, her voice echoing around the hall. '*Look away from their eyes, look away from their eyes, look away from their eyes.*'

Blane and Daisy looked on with admiration. Their fellow agent actually had a great voice!

'Believe in yourself, leave the CDs on the shelf, look away from their eyes, look away from their eyes, look away from their eyes.'

Rose was really getting into it. What had she been worried about? This was great! Completely carried away, Rose tossed off her Alice hairband, shaking her hair loose.

'Believe in only yourself, leave the CDs on the shelf, look away from their eyes.'

From up onstage, Rose watched in amazement as a change slowly came over the zombies scattered around the hall. Without exception, their eyes began to look a little less glazed over. Their rigid, upright bodies were loosening up.

Blane and Daisy were clapping along in delight. What's more, Gary, Arran and Darran were enjoying themselves onstage for the first time in ages. It was *such* a relief to play some new stuff without Tony Frisco breathing down their necks!

*Look away from their eyes,*
*Look away from their eyes,*
*Look away from their eyes*
*And you always will be free,*
*If you listen naturally.*

In the crowd, Rose's dad's head jerk back up straight as he looked around uncertainly. It wasn't long before he remembered where he was. He was in the St Hope's school hall – and there was his daughter up on stage, belting out a song!

Rose couldn't believe it. Her antidote was working! She was de-zombifying everyone. And not only that, she was rocking the house – even Mr Flatley was dancing.

> *Look away from their eyes,*
> *Look away from their eyes, look away . . .*

As Rose's lyrics came to an end there was a spontaneous and deafening burst of cheering and applause. Even her pop-hating parents joined in enthusiastically as Crush held their arms aloft in salute.

Rose stepped over to the side of the stage. Blane and Daisy gazed up at her with pride. Who would have thought their serious friend had the makings of a showbiz star?

'You were awesome!' Blane whooped.

'Really?' asked Rose, smiling humbly.

'Now that was *real* music!' he added, beaming.

Twenty minutes later, the three members of Crush were standing outside the school gates, preparing to get back on to their tour bus. The driver had finally managed to fix the alternator, which he figured must have come loose as the bus pulled in at St Hope's.

Blane and Rose were standing chatting to them.

'That was our best gig ever,' Gary was gushing. 'And it was all down to you, Rose – you *rock*!'

Rose felt herself blushing. She was warming to the band-member's charms – they really knew how to give a girl a compliment.

'Turns out we didn't need Mr Frisco's help after all,' Gary said, casting a nervous eye over Blane's shoulder. 'He's definitely gone, hasn't he?'

'Yeah,' Blane assured him with a smile. 'I promise you won't be seeing Tony Frisco again.'

'Here's a couple of complimentary tickets for tonight's gig,' Gary added, pulling two tickets out of his back pocket. 'Just don't give any to that kookie friend of yours, yeah?'

Gary's face clouded over as he spotted Daisy emerge waving from the building, flanked by Kaleigh and Zara.

'Er, we better be going,' he said hastily, disappearing on to the coach with Darran and Arran. 'We've got a tour to finish. Bye!'

The bus driver hurried in after the Crush boys clutching an *A–Z* and shut the doors, just as Daisy arrived.

'They still think I'm a crazy stalker, don't they?' she asked mournfully. Daisy felt like she'd completely blown it with her favourite band ever.

Rose and Blane looked away, trying hard to conceal their smiles. She'd be devastated when she heard about the tickets, but they could probably spare theirs after all.

\*   \*   \*

Not long after, Lenny summoned the M.I. High agents down to their headquarters. They were greeted with the sight of Tony Frisco sitting on a chair with a defeated expression on his face. He was still trapped inside the big bass drum.

'Well done, team!' Lenny nodded with satisfaction. 'The teenage zombie threat is over. Crush are going to be touring the UK – playing Rose's antidote song. And we've saved the world from cultural dictatorship.'

The agents grinned happily.

'Well, I've had enough of the tuba,' Rose said, changing the subject. 'I think I'll try something else.'

'Death metal?' asked Blane hopefully.

'Rap?' Daisy said helpfully.

Lenny instructed Frisco to stand and led him off to the lift.

'Good luck,' Blane shouted after him. 'You might be inside for a long time. Look at it this way – at least you can write some decent songs in there!'

Rose was true to her word about ditching the tuba and taking up another instrument. Later that week Blane and Daisy found themselves sitting in on one of her rehearsals with Ms Templeman.

Tina was still playing the violin, but this time Tanya was on the tuba.

'That's the something new she's taken up?' asked Daisy as she gazed at Rose's shiny instrument. 'The *clarinet*?'

Rose waved happily at her classmates. It was clear she was back to playing what she loved best – classical music.

Blane couldn't stop himself from smiling. He'd decided it was cool Rose played whatever she wanted. Just as long as it wasn't Crush!

He punched the air. 'Rock and roll!' he laughed.